THE GIRL IN WHITE

What's in a Name?

MERUPRANTA SAIKIA

INDIA · SINGAPORE · MALAYSIA

CONTENTS

CONTENTS

ABOUT THE AUTHOR

Merupranta Saikia is a passionate storyteller hailing from Assam, India. With an MBA from Tezpur University, he draws inspiration from personal experiences trying to incorporate them in his writings. His debut novel, *The Girl in White* explores the complexities of love, friendship, and the consequences of choices, weaving together a narrative that resonates with anyone who has faced the challenges of young adulthood.

An avid cricket fan, Merupranta Saikia often incorporates elements of the sport into his writing, blending the thrill of the game with deep emotional storytelling. When not writing, he enjoys gaming, exploring new cultures, and spending time with friends and family.

Merupranta Saikia currently resides in Mumbai where he is working at Hindustan Unilever Limited while continuing to share his love for writing.

ACKNOWLEDGEMENTS

This journey would not have been possible without the unwavering support of those closest to me.

To my parents, thank you for your endless love and encouragement. Your belief in me, even when I faltered, has been my greatest strength. You've been my guiding light, and I owe everything to the foundation you've provided.

To my friends, you have been my anchors through the highs and lows. Your unwavering support, late-night conversations, and constant motivation have kept me going, even when the road seemed long. I am beyond grateful for your presence in my life.

To the readers, thank you for choosing to spend your time with this story. Writing is a solitary journey, but the real magic happens when the words meet your eyes. I hope this book resonates with you and leaves a mark in your heart as it did in mine. Your time and attention are gifts I deeply cherish.

And to the characters within these pages, thank you for allowing me to tell your story. Though born from my imagination, you've guided me through this journey, teaching me more than I could have ever anticipated. I hope your stories live on in the hearts of those who read them.

PROLOGUE

It was an icy cold January morning, perhaps the coldest the month had seen. A new year had dawned, and with it, renewed hopes and fading resolutions. For most, it was the onset of the usual routines and humdrum existence, but for one soul, this day would become etched in memory forever.

The first day of a new term, the halls of the institution buzzed with the energy of a fresh academic term. Excitement, coupled with trepidation, hovered over the room as students settled into the unfamiliar desks. Amidst the mixed feelings of being away from home and the excitement of experiencing something new, the buzz inside the class suddenly seemed to come to a halt. Maybe it only struck me and not anyone else, or perhaps I had caught sight of someone who had the ability to freeze time. Moments earlier, I had settled into my seat, feeling overwhelmed by the new ambience—the unfamiliar desks, the blackboard, and the sea of unfamiliar faces. Amidst the casual scanning of the room, something remarkable happened—one that made me feel as though the world had come to a standstill; one that made my heart skip a beat.

At that moment, a face unlike any I had seen before appeared before my eyes. It was a girl who caught me off guard. Well, she was different, indeed. She strolled through the door towards her seat, oblivious to the effect she had on me. Earphones on, with hair falling just below her shoulders, she wore a pristine white sweater and a pair of old jeans, a stark contrast to the mundane palette of the classroom. Her very presence seemed to have breathed life into the monochrome surroundings, making everything else appear dull by comparison. She breezed past me, my gaze transfixed on her as if hypnotised by the snowy whiteness of her sweater, which mirrored the purity and allure of her enchanting face. In that moment, white became my favourite colour, and instantaneously she became *The Girl in White.*

"Time flies," they say, "when you are with the right person." I truly understood the precision of that saying once I looked at my watch. An hour had passed, and yet it felt like only a minute ago when she entered the classroom for the first time. I had been enchanted by her for an hour, and I felt reluctant to let the class end, yearning to relive the moment when she first graced the room. I knew nothing about her, not even her name, yet as I stepped out into the world, I carried a smile on my lips, a smile inspired by *The Girl in White.*

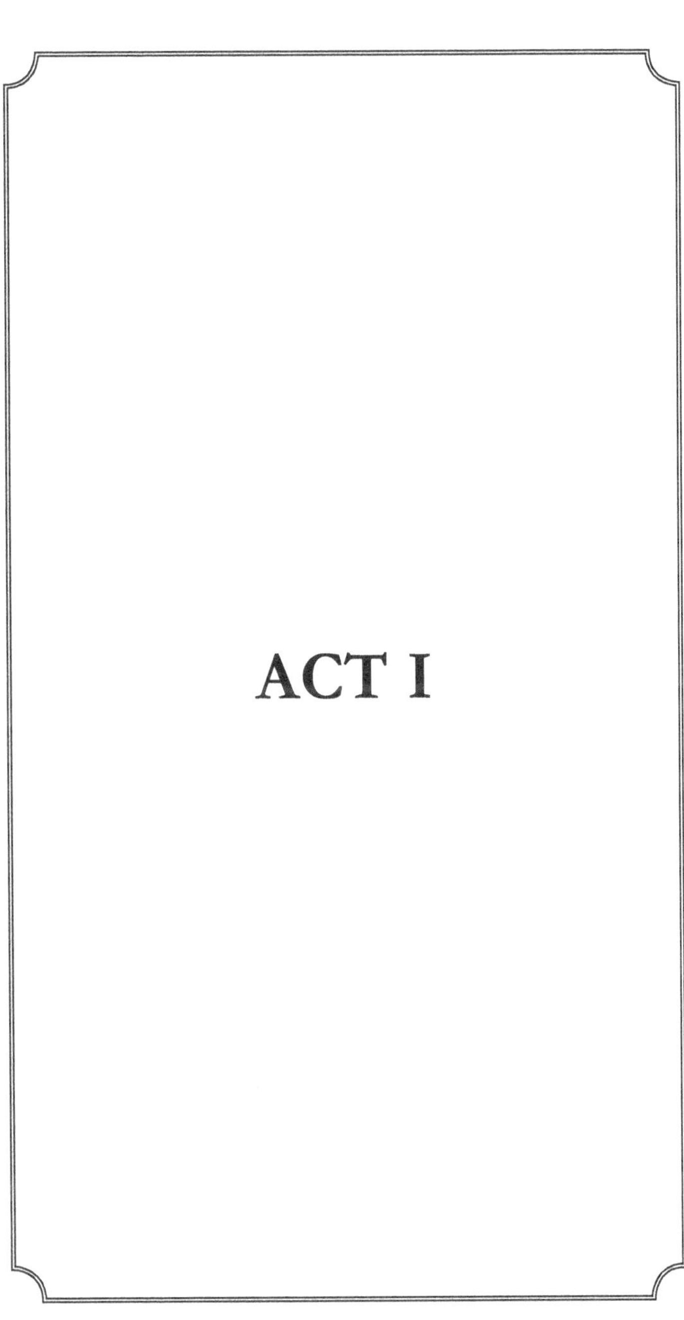

ACT I

Chapter 1

A NEW BEGINNING

"Excuse me, I think you dropped this," I heard someone call me from behind.

I turned around and saw a person standing with a notebook in his hand. He was rather short, and his hair was all over the place. He had a very thin stubble and was wearing a blue T-shirt. He smiled at me and handed me the notebook that I had left inside the classroom.

"Oh, thanks!" I said with a hint of anxiety.

"I am Prachurjya," he smiled and extended his hand.

"I am Madhav. Nice to meet you," I replied, shaking his hand.

"Where are you from?" he said.

"I am from Guwahati," I replied.

"Guwahati!" he exclaimed. "Nice."

I nodded, feeling slightly awkward but didn't say much.

"This place seems really nice, doesn't it?" Prachurjya remarked.

"I guess," I replied.

"Where are you from?" I inquired.

"Jorhat," he beamed.

"Have you ever been there?" Prachurjya asked.

I shook my head and could instantly feel his face twitch slightly.

"Okay, I'll see you later, and thank you for returning the notebook." I said as the conversation reached a lull.

"Sure thing!" Prachurjya grinned.

This was my first real interaction in the university, apart from the brief exchange with the student who shared his notebook for me to fill in the notes I had missed in the previous class. I had been so preoccupied with the mysterious girl from the previous class that I did not notice anyone else.

The break was short, and soon I found myself in a different classroom, surrounded by new faces once again. However, all my attention was devoted to scanning the room in search of the mysterious girl, but she was nowhere to be found.

"Mind if I sit here?" a girl's voice interrupted my thoughts. "All the other seats are taken."

I turned towards her, hoping it was the mysterious girl, but it wasn't. This girl had long, straight black hair that ended just below her waist. She was wearing a pair of square-shaped glasses that she kept readjusting. She carried three large books in her tiny arms; they were almost the size of telephone directories. She reminded me of a studious girl from my school days who aced every exam there possibly was.

"Sure," I replied, feeling somewhat dejected.

"Thanks," she said with a nod.

"Hello," I tried to strike up a conversation after a few seconds.

"Hi," she responded without looking at me, engrossed in her books.

She seemed busy, but my curiosity got the better of me.

"Excuse me," I said gently. "I notice a lot of new faces in this class. Faces that were nowhere to be seen in the last class. It's not what I expected. Do you have an idea why?"

Her response was rather cold.

"Expected?"

"Perhaps you did not check your schedule, did you?"

I shook my head, feeling slightly embarrassed.

"The first class was an optional session where students from other batches who share an interest in German join us. It is supposed to happen only thrice a week," she explained in a somewhat bossy tone.

"WHAT? That was the German class?" I exclaimed.

She widened her eyes in disbelief.

"You really didn't pick up on that? Did you expect to hear *ich bin gut* and *was machst du* all day?"

Trying not to embarrass myself anymore, I laughed.

"I was just kidding. Of course, it was the German class."

"Right," she smirked. "Do you even know what *'was machst du'* means?"

I looked puzzled, and just then, the professor entered the room, saving me from further embarrassment.

The class began, and the bespectacled girl beside me rapidly transcribed everything the professor said. I couldn't help but be amazed by her speed. At times, I felt as though the professor had to catch up to her and that the professor was dictating later, and she was writing first.

Suddenly, it occurred to me that I hadn't asked her name, and I did want to ask her, but it didn't seem like the right idea to interrupt her.

"So, the next German class is two days away," I thought.

"It's okay," I reassured myself, thinking, "I'll see her again on Friday."

Yet, Friday still felt like an eternity away, and I couldn't shake the feeling that those two days would be the longest two days ever.

Chapter 2

MY FIRST FRIENDS

"*The Inter-Hostel Cricket Tournament starts in the first week of February. The hostel team is looking for new talent, and trials begin this Saturday at 4:00 p.m. Those interested are asked to submit their names in the drop box of the hostel and report on time,*" read the hostel's notice board the next morning.

"Finally, something to be excited about other than my German classes," I sighed. Cricket had been my passion since childhood. I had played it incessantly from the age of six, and my mother would often have to drag me off the field even as twilight fell.

Breakfast was served in a massive hall, where boarders formed queues at one end to receive their meals. Seniors often jumped the line. Not wanting any trouble, I moved to the left side, grabbed a plate, and waited for my turn. The morning rush gave everyone a hurried appearance, as if they were racing against time. After finishing, I left my plate at the sink and hurried to the department building, which was about half a mile away. By the time I arrived, the classroom was already packed with students, all chatting and making friends. I still hadn't truly gotten to know anyone.

Then I spotted the bespectacled girl from the previous day. I, however, didn't know her name.

"Unless you want to stand there staring, take a seat," she spoke in a bossy tone without looking at me.

"Sure," I mumbled, taking the seat next to her. She pulled out a large book, similar to the ones she had the day before.

"By the way, I am Madhav, and you are...?" I tried to break the ice.

She paused, then smiled.

"I am Ritika, from Kolkata."

"Oh, from the land of the Bengal Tiger," I chuckled, only to realise my mistake. She shot me a sharp look.

"Why are you always so nervous?" she then asked, turning a page from her enormous book.

"No, I am not," I said nervously.

She shook her head.

Meanwhile, the professor had walked in and begun the lecture. As the class had settled, the door banged open suddenly, causing Ritika to nearly drop her pen in shock. It was Prachurjya, the guy I had met the other day, panting and breathless.

"Ma'am... I... am... sorry... Late breakfast," he stammered.

The professor shook her head in disgust, looking at him as though he had committed treason.

"Set an alarm next time!" she said fiercely. "I'll let you in this time, but only this time."

"Thank you, ma'am," he said, marching toward the empty seat beside me. I suddenly found myself sandwiched between Ritika and Prachurjya.

"Why the fuss? I was only a couple of minutes late," Prachurjya mumbled. "As if being two minutes late is the end of the world."

"You were fifteen minutes late, not two. 'A couple' means two." Ritika corrected him.

"I thought I was talking to him, not you. Minding one's business is clearly out of fashion these days," he muttered.

"Not when you mistake fifteen minutes for two," she said coolly.

"Shh," I intervened.

"She is a bit crazy, isn't she?" Prachurjya whispered after a few seconds of silence.

"Umm... I am not sure," I said, trying not to move my lips.

"Apparently, honesty isn't common anymore," he said.

The professor threw us a sharp look but continued the lesson.

"Of course, she has the right to rebuke you for being late," I said after a moment.

"No," Prachurjya squealed. "I was talking about Ritika, not her."

"Are you crazy too?" he said, letting out a giant laugh.

Unfortunately, it was loud enough for the professor to overhear, and this time she lost her patience. Before we knew it, we were thrown out of class, with our attendance struck off.

My college experience was going from bad to worse.

"Thanks," I said sarcastically as we loitered aimlessly in the corridors.

"It wasn't my fault. I wasn't that loud," he defended himself.

"Right," I smirked. "Let's head downstairs to the canteen," I suggested, trying to shift the topic. "We still have half an hour before the next class."

Prachurjya's eyes lit up, and he started walking pompously.

The corridors were unusually deserted since everyone was in their classrooms except for us. The canteen on the other hand, was filled with students, many waiting in line for food or notes to be photocopied. Most of them were the ones who had skipped their first class or had classes off.

"Lucky, they don't have to rush early to class," Prachurjya said.

"Lucky they weren't thrown out of class first thing in the morning," I sneered.

Prachurjya looked at me and laughed again, like the laugh that had gotten us thrown out of class.

I shook my head, unsure what to say.

Though it seemed unlikely that we would find an empty table, we luckily managed to find one just vacated by a departing group. I glanced at my watch, then made my way to the counter. After a long wait in line, I ordered two cold drinks.

"Forty rupees," the man at the counter said.

I paid the bill and, as I slid my wallet back into my pocket, my elbow brushed against someone's arm, sending a jolt of electricity through me. I turned, and once again, time seemed to freeze. It was her—*The Girl in White*. She stood in the line beside me, surrounded by friends, yet somehow completely apart.

My ears went red, and my heart raced faster than a supercar.

"Your order… Hello!" the man at the counter called repeatedly before I snapped back to reality.

"Yes," I replied, dazed, grabbing the drinks and heading back to our table. I didn't look back and hoped I wouldn't trip because my legs had turned extremely shaky.

"Finally, you are here. What took you so long?" Prachurjya asked, stirring his drink with a straw.

"Nothing, the queue was too long," I replied, my gaze drifting as I craned my neck to catch a glimpse of her. She sat about thirty metres away, captivating in a way that made it impossible for me to look anywhere else.

"I am not sure you know, but you are supposed to drink this, not let it sit until it turns hot," Prachurjya said after some time.

"What?" I replied, confused.

He sighed, possibly annoyed by my lack of attention to his humour. I ignored him and kept looking for her.

"CAN IT POSSIBLY BE LOVE?" I thought.

"No," a voice inside me responded. "It has only been two days; you need to stop thinking so much."

"But what do you know about love? She might just be the one," argued another voice.

Just then, Ritika stormed into the canteen. Her class had just ended.

"I knew you two would be here," Ritika said.

"But how and why are you here looking for us?" Prachurjya asked as he took a sip of his cold drink.

"Because you called me crazy," she growled. "And next time, try not to get thrown out of class."

"It wasn't my fault," I said, looking away.

"Oh yes, of course," Prachurjya said, looking disgusted. "It was all my fault. Blame it on me."

"Correct," I said.

Prachurjya shook his head and took a sip from his drink.

Ritika meanwhile had ordered a cup of coffee so dark it looked like it could keep someone awake for a month.

"What is this abomination you are drinking?" Prachurjya exclaimed in disgust.

I laughed.

Ritika ignored us both and downed the coffee in one go.

"Kids these days," she mumbled.

"Hurry up," she said, adjusting her glasses. "It is almost time for the next class. Try not to get thrown out again."

"Keep that in mind, Prachurjya," I said.

The three of us laughed together.

Prachurjya and I returned the empty bottles, and Ritika disposed of her paper cup. As we made our way out of the canteen, I craned my neck one last time to look at the table where *The Girl in White* had been sitting—only to find it empty, she was gone.

"Friday then," I thought to myself, heading to class alongside Ritika and Prachurjya.

Chapter 3

WHAT'S IN A NAME?

The morning's alarm buzzed loudly, jolting me awake. I fumbled to silence it and squinted at my phone. A few notifications, including a text from Prachurjya flashed on the screen:

"Drop by when you are up. Breakfast together."

Glancing at the time, I saw it was 8:15 AM, giving me precisely one hour before the first class.

I crawled out of bed, my mind gradually shaking off the remnants of sleep. Then it hit me—it was Friday. Excitement coursed through my veins; Fridays meant our German class, and I would get to see her again for an entire hour—the one who had so effortlessly stolen my heart.

I hurriedly dressed in my favourite T-shirt, applied more cologne than ever before, donned sneakers that looked pearly white, and spent five minutes meticulously combing my hair before rushing towards the hall.

But first, I had to go see Prachurjya. Since his room was downstairs, I had to navigate through two floors and three wings to reach him. Knocking on his door, I called his name, but there was no response.

I tried again, a bit louder this time. Finally, the door cracked open, but standing there was not Prachurjya, but a guy I had seen around only a few times before. Though we had never spoken before, I recognised him. He was Prachurjya's roommate. He was rather thin with an unkempt moustache.

"Good morning!" he said.

I nodded.

Apparently, he had been getting ready for his class as well.

"Where is Prachurjya?" I inquired.

"He has gone to the washroom; should be back soon," he replied.

"Okay," I said and decided to wait for him, albeit impatiently.

A few moments later, he arrived, got dressed instantaneously and dragged me to the breakfast hall. Prachurjya was sporting his blue T-shirt for the third consecutive day, while his roommate had donned a neatly pressed blue chequered shirt tucked into black trousers.

"What's our first class today?" Prachurjya asked.

"German," I replied with a grin.

"Not again," he groaned.

"Why are you so excited? By the way, this is my roommate, Biswajyoti. He is our classmate too."

"We are classmates," Biswajyoti corrected.

"I know; we met," I replied hastily, eager to sidestep the previous question.

The three of us then reached the breakfast hall, had breakfast, and then made our way to the classroom. My strides were longer than usual, and with each step, the restlessness further intensified. My heart raced, and I kept on checking my watch just to ensure I was not late by even a single second.

"Relax," I reminded myself a couple of times. "Act normal."

Once we reached inside the classroom, I spotted Ritika and sat next to her while Prachurjya took a seat behind us. I discreetly glanced around the room, searching for her but found no sign of *The Girl in White*. I assumed she hadn't arrived yet and eagerly waited for the moment when she would walk across that door once again.

"Looking for someone?" Ritika asked suddenly, catching me off guard.

"Me? No, not at all," I replied nervously.

She gave me an odd look, then turned her attention to the front of the classroom. As I counted the minutes, the anxiety built up within me. I couldn't help but feel restless.

"What if she didn't show up? Would I have to wait for another three days to see her again? Did she opt out of the optional subject?"

My mind raced with a million thoughts. I was anxious and kept craning my neck towards the door in hopes that she would arrive soon.

After a few minutes, the door, which had been left ajar, was pushed open, and she walked in—the one I had been waiting to see for so long. Her entrance brought a wave of calm, and I was instantly enchanted all over again. She seemed even more beautiful, and once again, I felt completely bewitched by her presence. It was almost as if she had cast a spell over me. My head turned as she glided past me, leaving me utterly dumbstruck.

I tried to soak in the entire moment like it was the only moment I had been waiting for in my life, but I realised that someone had been looking at me. I turned my head towards Ritika, and she stared at me, looking both amused and perplexed at the same time.

"What?" I said.

"Why are you looking at me like that?"

"I wouldn't have if you had not been staring at that girl in the first place," she replied.

"No, I was not... It's just that…" I tried to save face, but just then, like last time, the door swung open again, and this time too, the Professor entered.

"Thank goodness," I sighed inwardly.

As the rest of the class settled in, my eagerness continued to mount. I wanted to catch another glimpse of her, but Ritika's actions made me think twice. I rolled my eyes to the left once or twice without turning my head, but with little luck.

"Should have been a rabbit," I thought. "At least that way, I could have looked at her without turning my head."

In an attempt to steal a glance at her, I dropped my pen. As I bent down to pick it up, my eyes fell on her. She was gazing intently at the professor, nodding occasionally, looking as beautiful as ever.

"If only I could freeze time," I thought, utterly captivated by her, still looking at her from below.

"Is there a problem there?" the professor suddenly asked, her gaze fixed on me.

Heads turned, including hers, as I raised my head from below the desk, lifted the pen, and stood up to face the professor. My cheeks flushed; the last thing I wanted was to embarrass myself in front of that mysterious girl.

"Uh, no, ma'am," I fumbled.

"Then be seated normally!" she said, and she continued with her lecture.

I glanced at Ritika, who remained silent. I vowed not to move until the end of the class.

"She noticed you," I silently acknowledged and smiled. "Not the best first impression, but at least something."

Ritika seemed too busy taking notes, and Prachurjya, on the other hand, was sitting lazily on his bench, too bored to listen to anything the professor had to say. With the end of the hour, the professor concluded the class, and most of the class was busy packing their books into their bags. Suddenly, something happened that made my ears prick up.

"Kuhi, canteen, right?" I heard a girl speak, who was sitting two rows behind me.

"Yes, of course," she replied in the gentlest manner. It was the first time I had heard her voice.

"Oh, the calmness in her voice," I thought.

"Kuhi! She has an even prettier name," I whispered, with a giant smile on my face.

"What?" Ritika suddenly spoke.

"What?" I turned towards her, fearing she heard what I said.

"No, I thought you said something," she replied, looking confused.

I shrugged.

The bell rang, and I hurriedly packed my bags.

"Why do you always seem so lost?" Ritika asked as we walked out of the class.

Kuhi's name kept ringing in my ears, and I was uninterested in anything else happening around me

"Sorry?" I replied.

"Ah, see! This is what I was talking about… You always seem so lost," she said and looked away.

"Who were you looking at in the class today, if I may ask?"

I almost let out a gasp. I was not quite sure what to say.

"Nobody," I said at once. "You are imagining things."

"Not in the mood to tell, well, we will soon find out."

"Wanna go grab something to eat?" Prachurjya suggested.

With no more classes scheduled, we were mostly free.

"We can. What do you think, Ritika?" I asked, even though a part of me wanted to rush to the canteen, but I soon realised that would not be a good idea.

"I am in," she replied.

"The last one to arrive pays the bill," Prachurjya declared, clearly excited, and dashed outside. Ritika and I chuckled at his enthusiasm.

"What a character," she commented.

I laughed.

"What's in a name?" I had often wondered. But in that moment, I realised there is everything in a name. *Kuhi* was more than just a word. Those four letters had suddenly taken on a significance far deeper than I had ever imagined.

"What would you like?" Ritika asked once we reached the restaurant.

"Kuhi!" I silently exclaimed in my mind.

But out loud, I simply said, "Bread and eggs, of course."

Chapter 4

THE TEST OF SKILL

The next morning, I woke up earlier than usual. It was the day of the trials for the Inter-Hostel tournament. I had captained my school team, was also part of my college team, and I could not wait to make my way into the University team. Therefore, being part of this tournament was crucial to achieving that goal.

Prachurjya, Biswajyoti, and I took our usual walk to the Dining Hall. The three of us had made it a habit to have our meals together.

"Ready to smash some big sixes?" Prachurjya asked me during our breakfast.

"I would rather prefer to rattle the stumps," I replied while peeling the shell of an egg.

"I haven't bowled in a while, though."

I had always been more of a bowler, a fast bowler to be exact. The thrill of releasing the ball, watching it curve and deceive in mid-air, and the satisfying sound of the ball hitting the timber brought me immense joy. While I could handle the bat, it was bowling that truly excited me.

"Good luck, bro," Prachurjya said between bites of bread, while Biswajyoti simply enjoyed his morning tea.

After breakfast, I went back to my room and sorted out my cricket kit. Even though I had taken a break from the sport, I felt positive and confident. After all, this was just the hostel team trials.

"Do well here, and you will be one step closer to the University team," I reminded myself.

At exactly half past nine, I double-checked my kit and headed to the ground. It was a massive field divided into two sections. On one side, football players dashed around, trying to score goals, while on the other side, cricketers in white jerseys and hats were waiting for their turn. A pathway separated the two, a place for people to stroll and admire the view in the evenings. The towering floodlights made it one of the best cricket grounds in the vicinity.

Although I had been to the ground a couple of times since joining the university, this was my first time there as a player.

About forty eager players from the first year had shown up for the trials, just like me, hoping to make the cut. All of us were eager to come out on top.

After a ten-minute wait, a tall, sturdy figure arrived, carrying a pair of pads and a helmet. He was accompanied by a few players who looked like they belonged to the hostel team. It was clear that this tall guy was the captain of the team.

"Thanks for being punctual," he said, placing the pads gently on the ground. "I am Anuj, your potential teammate and captain. We will practise hard over the next few weeks to be ready to play our best."

I could see that spark in his eyes that marked a leader.

"Remember, a good performance in this tournament could get you closer to the University team too," he added.

His words fuelled my motivation, and I couldn't wait to get started.

"All right then," he announced. "Batsmen on the left, pacers on the right, and spinners will bowl in tandem," he directed. "Let's begin. Give it your best shot, guys."

I nodded in agreement and joined the group on the right, consisting of about nine pace bowlers. I warmed up, waiting anxiously for my turn to bowl.

After fifteen minutes of warming up, the first pair completed their overs, and then, it was my turn. I marked my run-up and charged toward the batsman. My first delivery was a short ball, and the batsman ducked skilfully.

"Come on, pitch it up," Anuj shouted from a distance. "This will not fetch you any wickets."

I went back, took a few steps, ran with all my might and delivered the next ball. It left my fingers smoothly, kissed the surface, and a split second later, I heard the satisfying thud as the off stump was sent cartwheeling about a metre and a half from its original position.

"Absolute peach of a delivery," Anuj exclaimed with delight. "Well done! That line and length was almost unplayable."

I was on cloud nine, having dismissed the batsman with a brilliant delivery. I returned to complete my over and managed to touch the edges of the bat twice during that spell.

I was happy with my performance, and I joined the rest of the group, waiting for their turns.

I waited there anxiously, occasionally fetching a few balls that managed to sneak out of the nets.

As the session ended, we gathered near the dressing room; tension and anticipation filled the air.

"Great job, everyone. While most of you performed well, remember that we can only select a few. We have shortlisted five names we believe deserve to make the cut," Anuj said.

"Don't be disheartened if you are not selected. One mediocre session does not define your calibre. But since this is the only way possible considering the tight schedule and requirements of the team, this is what we must be content with for the moment."

My heart raced. Despite being confident of my chances, the realisation that only five players would be chosen from the lot dwindled my confidence to an extent.

"Jayanta, we need a solid left-handed batsman, and you seem just the right player to fill that spot. You are in," Anuj revealed.

"Try not to rush into playing rash shots, and you will do wonders."

Jayanta was indeed a talented batsman, who could effortlessly hit boundaries and score quick runs.

He joined the team with a grin as we all clapped.

"Bhaskar, you showed us that you can move the ball both ways. You are in too," Anuj added.

Bhaskar cheered with delight, thrilled to make the team.

"Uttam, a leg spinner is a valuable asset to any team, and we want you to be that asset for us. Welcome to the team," Anuj continued, leading to applause for Uttam.

"Congratulations, Kushal. Your solid batting technique impressed us. You are in as well."

My heart started beating faster. There was only one spot left and an entire pool of players.

"And finally, Madhav, we think you are a natural. You have good pace, and the way you bowled today, it looked as if you had great belief in your abilities too. We hope you can carry this forward and put on a good show," he said. "Welcome to the team."

I was delighted, and I nodded at Anuj as a sign of gratitude.

"See you all next Saturday," he said and left the ground.

I was elated by my selection and flashed a wide smile at Anuj. As I hoisted my kit onto my shoulder, I made my way back to the hostel, playfully knocking my bat.

"I didn't need your services today, my friend. Perhaps next week," I said, putting my cricket bat inside my kit as I unlocked my room.

Chapter 5

THE BABYSTEPS

It was an overcast Sunday morning. The sky hung heavy with dull grey clouds, casting a sombre shadow over the day. Occasional gusts of wind rattled the glass pane of my almost broken window, creating an eerie, almost haunted atmosphere. With heavy eyelids, I tossed the thin blanket to the other end of the bed and dragged myself upright.

I reached for my phone and dialled Prachurjya's number. It took him about a minute to answer my call. In a groggy voice, indicative of deep slumber, he mumbled, "Hello."

"Hey, I was thinking—would you like to go out? We could have breakfast somewhere else," I asked, hoping for a positive response. I had grown tired of the bland hostel food.

"What is the time?" he asked even more sluggishly, still struggling to wake up.

"It's ten-thirty already," I replied, emphasising the lateness. "Get up before our breakfast plan turns into an outing for lunch."

"I am sleeping for another half an hour," he protested. "Food and sleep should complement each other. Why choose one over the other?" he said, letting out a big yawn.

"Please, will you stop? Get ready in fifteen minutes; I am coming to your room," I said, while squeezing the last bit of toothpaste from the tube.

About twenty minutes later, I arrived at his room and knocked on the door. It was Biswajyoti once again who answered, while Prachurjya was still fast asleep. I marched towards him and pulled his blanket tightly away from him.

"I gave you twenty minutes to get ready, and here you are, still snoring like a pig," I said.

"Breakfast and sleep should comp—"

"Complement each other!" Biswajyoti chimed in. "This is the fourth time he has said this since I tried waking him up," Biswajyoti chuckled.

"I think I have a solution to this adversity," I said. I hurried towards his messy study table and grabbed the giant water bottle. His eyes widened in horror.

"Get ready to have a bath while in bed, Mr. Sleepyhead," I said.

"Don't even try," Prachurjya roared out loud.

In about half a second, he leaped out of bed and jolted out of the room. "Here is your toothbrush and towel," I said, tossing his belongings towards him.

"I am not going to forget this," he shouted while running towards the bathroom.

"I am sure," I said.

As we waited for Prachurjya to return, I pulled out my phone and began swiping through various apps. Then, a thought crossed my mind, causing my eyes to light up instantly. "Why didn't I think of it before?" I wondered.

With fingers that glided like an aircraft, I searched for her on *Facebook*. I typed '*K-U-H-I*', and as soon as I pressed the search button, her name appeared right at the top. My heart leaped with delight. Without a second thought, I visited her profile and clicked on the picture that appeared on the homepage.

The screen illuminated from the image of her profile. It was an image I could not tear my eyes away from—her in that same white sweater from our first encounter. Every detail of the photo was etched in my mind. Her eyes seemed to hold a world of secrets, and her smile radiated a warmth that transcended the digital barrier. In that moment, I felt like a man possessed, captivated by this digital representation of her ethereal existence. It was an infatuation I could not explain, yet it held me captive.

I was so deeply engrossed in her photo that I didn't even notice when Prachurjya returned. It was only when he said, "Do you have a problem with your vision?" that I realised he was back. I quickly stashed my phone in my pocket and stood up.

"Yes," I said sarcastically, trying to dodge the situation. "Now get ready."

He shook his head in disappointment and started singing while getting ready. Once he had gotten ready, we made our way outside. The gate was a five-minute walk from our hostel, and Prachurjya started making small talk. He had a never-ending list of topics, and I only responded when he asked me something. Most of my replies were limited to "*Yes,*" "*Um-hmmm,*" and "*Of course.*"

We reached the restaurant, and during our five-minute journey, my mind was consumed by thoughts of Kuhi and the profile I had checked earlier.

"Do you have a girlfriend?" Prachurjya asked casually, flipping through the menu.

I glanced at him and, after a brief pause, replied, "No... Do you?"

He gave me a penetrating look and then burst into laughter. "LOL," he said.

I raised my eyebrows and shook my head. By then, I had gotten used to his weird behaviour and responses. I chose to ignore him and unlocked my phone. Her profile appeared on the screen once more.

"There is no harm in sending her a friend request; it's just a friend request," I thought. But then, doubt crept in. "What if she rejects my request? We've barely talked, and she doesn't even know me."

I was locked in a battle of 'yes' and 'no' in my mind, a battle that could be decided with the press of a button. On one hand, the prospect of sending a friend request to Kuhi was alluring. Yet, on the other, the fear of rejection loomed large. We had barely exchanged words, and she was essentially a stranger. What if she dismissed my request with a click? It was a dilemma that tugged at my heart, leaving me hesitant.

"What a dilemma," I sighed while staring at my screen.

"Why are you always so lost?" Prachurjya asked me suddenly. This was the first time he looked serious since the time I had known him. I was surprised, for Ritika had asked me the same question a few days back.

"Ritika, is that you disguised as Prachurjya?" I joked.

He flinched so hard at this that he knocked the bottle of salt to the ground. The owner of the restaurant gave him a sharp look but instantly looked away.

"But do I?" I asked him rather seriously.

Just as he was about to answer, our breakfast arrived. I ordered an *aloo paratha* and a glass of milk, while Prachurjya chose noodles and poached eggs. I was starving, and it took me less than two minutes to finish my meal, almost devouring all of it.

Prachurjya, however, took his time, enjoying every bite as though it were a meal from a five-star hotel.

Afterward, we headed to a nearby store where Prachurjya bought a couple of cigarettes. He offered me one, but I declined. He lit a cigarette and began smoking.

"I am surprised you said no. Never smoked one?" he asked, taking a puff.

"Not really," I said, looking at him with a tone of pride in my voice.

"Why?" he asked.

"How can there be a 'why' to this?" I laughed. He looked bemused.

"Lost a potential cigarette partner," he joked. "No free midnight cigarettes for me then."

I shot him a flustered look.

"Let's get going," he said after finishing his cigarette, extinguishing it with his foot before paying the shopkeeper.

We walked back to our hostel for another three minutes. Just as we were about to reach our hostel, I felt a familiar jolt in my body. I stopped walking while Prachurjya kept on talking without noticing anything. I had caught sight of her again. The fourth time, and I was still in awe of her just like the first time I had seen her.

I did not expect to see her, but I did. She had a book in her hand, and just like our first encounter, she had her earphones on. She did not notice me and walked straight past as though I were invisible. I turned around, hoping she would do the same, but I quickly realised that such things only happened in movies.

It took me a moment to compose myself, and I only started walking once she was at a considerable distance from where I stood. I increased my pace to catch up with Prachurjya. As I reached nearer to him, I realised he was still talking oblivious to what had happened. We reached our hostel, and during the entire way, I just kept thinking about her.

"So, we are going tomorrow then?" Prachurjya said as we entered the entrance of our hostel.

"Eh, what?" I said. I had not listened to anything Prachurjya had been blabbering since the time we came back.

"Weirdo!" he exclaimed, walking coolly towards his room, and I followed suit. Upon reaching his room, we found Biswajyoti sitting with another guy named Ashish, who was also in our class and a friend of Biswajyoti.

"Hi, Madhav," Ashish greeted me. "I heard you went for breakfast."

"Oh, hi. Yeah, Prachurjya and I decided to eat out," I replied, a bit surprised.

"How come we've never had the chance to talk?" Ashish asked, a hint of mystery in his tone. "I am glad that's all about to change."

"Yeah, definitely," I said in a perplexed tone. He kept on looking at me ominously for some time, and once the room had turned oddly silent, I spoke.

"Prachurjya, I have a pile of clothes that need washing. I'll see you at lunch," I said as I left his room.

"Bye, Biswajyoti. Bye, Ashish," I called out on my way out.

"Bye, Madhav," Ashish replied loudly.

Once I reached my room, I lay on my bed, surprised by Ashish's unusual behaviour. I pulled out my phone again, the screen illuminating her profile. I found myself grappling with similar thoughts. It was just a touch on the screen, yet sometimes even the simplest action, like clicking a button, felt daunting.

I recalled someone saying that facing a lion required a lion's heart. Perhaps that person had never experienced love because, at times, even the smallest touch on a screen could be more intimidating than confronting a hungry lion.

But in that moment, I summoned my courage, closed my eyes, took a deep breath, and with a resolute tap, sent the friend request. It was a small action, a mere click of a button, yet it felt like conquering a formidable fear.

"Friend Request Sent" flashed on the screen, and with it came a rush of exhilaration and anxiety, knowing I had taken this decisive step. This was my leap of faith, a small stride towards a hopeful connection.

"Things we do for love," I muttered, a line I had picked up from some movie. I then set aside my phone and hurried towards the community washing machine with a bucketful of clothes in hand.

Chapter 6

A SPECIAL BOND

Anxiety, restlessness, nervousness, and edginess—these four emotions perfectly encapsulated my state of mind in the days following the sent *'friend request'*. My phone had become my constant companion, accompanying me everywhere from my bed to the dining hall. Each time I unlocked it, its screen illuminated with hope that Kuhi might have accepted my request. Each time I unlocked it, there was a rush of excitement and anticipation, only to be followed by mild disappointment as no notification appeared. This routine became my daily mantra, turning my phone into both a beacon of hope and a symbol of unmet expectations.

Days after I had sent the request, I unlocked it again. Yet, no such notification arrived that day, or the day following, or even the week that followed. I saw less of her other than the class hours that happened just thrice a week, and only once did I manage to catch a glimpse of her in the canteen. I often thought about retracting the request to rid myself of the discomfort, but hesitation always held me back.

"Is something on your mind?" Ritika's observant eyes caught the subtle shifts in my behaviour one day as we strolled along the corridors.

"No, not really... Why do you ask?" I said, clearing my throat. Her gaze remained unwavering. "I have been observing you for a few days, and you seem to be glued to your phone, as if awaiting something, or someone."

"Quite the observer, Miss Sherlock.", I said.

"However useless it may be," a chuckle escaped me.

"You are impossible," she sighed in disappointment.

I chose to disregard her remark, unlocking my phone once more. Two seconds later, I found her looking at me with absolute disdain, and the two of us burst into laughter together.

"However useless it may be," she teased, mimicking me. Hearing this, I burst out with laughter once again, and so did Ritika.

"See… so much better when you do not hold yourself back," she said jubilantly once we reached our classroom and smiled.

"We have become quite the pair, haven't we?" I said, savouring the lighter moment once the class had ended.

"Indeed," Ritika agreed with a smile.

"But sometimes it's better to talk, you know. Not holding back really helps," she commented.

I smiled in return.

"Sometimes, indeed." I said.

As the warning bell for the next class rang, she dragged me towards our next classroom, holding me by my arm.

"God… Ritika, you have a firm grip," I said while examining my arm for any signs of fracture.

"Stop being a dainty doll," she said ferociously.

We headed to our classroom, riding the wave of shared laughter and friendship. In the days that followed, routine classes resumed, as did rigorous cricket practice. My focus shifted to the impending tournament. There were still no signs of any notification, and once the practice had kicked off, I barely had any time to check my phone, for we had to undergo intense practice both on Saturdays and Sundays.

The tournament was fast approaching, and it was essential to leave no stone unturned. Anuj, our captain, worked tirelessly to prepare us, moulding the team to perfection.

I had been bowling consistently well, and it seemed that I had impressed Anuj.

"We have high expectations from you," he told me one day during practice. "But remember, never become complacent."

A nod and a smile were my responses.

I could not afford to disappoint him or the team. One Sunday, I was given a chance to bat as well. While not a very prominent batsman, I could send the ball over the boundaries when the opportunity arose. In the practice nets, I faced twenty-four balls. A few big hits and two dismissals were the result. Anuj approached me, acknowledging my efforts but cautioning me against throwing away my wicket.

"Remember, you may be a key bowler, but you are not in any way exempted from giving your all with the bat. It might come down to you to secure a victory, so be ready when the opportunity presents itself," he emphasised.

Anuj's words lingered in my mind, sparking determination to perform well, not only as a bowler but also as a batsman; after all, cricket is played with both bat and ball.

"Meet me at the juice shop after practice," Anuj said while we were busy packing the kit bags. Although I had plans to join Prachurjya and Ritika post-practice, I could not decline Anuj's proposal.

As the sun set, we agreed to meet for the final session on Friday, the day before our first Inter-Hostel match. The upcoming match against the *Nilachal Men's Hostel* weighed heavily on our minds, a rivalry spanning years.

Anuj and I went to the nearest juice shop in the shopping complex of the university. The juice shop was stationed at the corner of the complex. A man who looked like he was in his mid-forties attended to us politely.

"What would you like to have?" he said to us. I ordered a glass of watermelon juice and a bowl of fruit salad. Anuj had a large pomegranate juice.

"You do know that the match next week is very important," Anuj said once he had finished drinking the juice.

"Yes, I do; as a matter of fact, all the matches are…" I said while sipping the juice.

"I mean I am aware of this on-field rivalry with them, but then, it is only a matter of doing what is right on the given day, and I am sure results will come our way irrespective of who we play," I said coolly.

Anuj looked at me and smiled.

"I see so much of myself in you when I was your age," he said.

"I came here four years ago, and this, of course, as you know, is my final year."

I could sense a bit of disappointment in his voice.

"We have not really been able to beat *Nilachal Men's Hostel* for almost four years now; not once since I joined the team."

"I would get no greater joy than to taste victory in my final tournament against them and then if all goes well, lift the trophy too."

I nodded as he spoke with passion.

"We had almost done it two years ago; we only needed nine runs off the last over with one wicket in hand. I was batting on sixty-four, and I had managed to take it to two runs needed off one ball. I could have easily played it down the ground, but I decided to go for a heroic shot and hit it over covers. As the ball flew into the air, my heart sank for I knew I had hit it straight to the fielder at the ropes. He caught it, and we lost by one run."

"I could have won it for the team, but I threw my wicket away, and believe me, this has been one of my biggest regrets," he said in a remorseful tone. "And this is exactly why I ask you to not throw your wicket away."

"I really hope we can pull out a victory this time, and believe me when I say this, you are going to play a pivotal part in that," he said and thumped his glass on the table with utmost enthusiasm.

The owner of the shop almost clapped at his passionate speech but was also concerned if the thud had broken his glass. It appeared he was as much engaged in Anuj's story as I.

As always, I was at a loss for words.

"You know what… Everything will go our way, trust me," I said finally and beamed at him.

"Absolutely," he said in a rejoiced tone.

"Unless, of course, you choose to throw your wicket away," he chuckled.

"Not happening any time soon," I said and got up.

We left the juice shop, and in about ten minutes, we reached our hostel. We exchanged goodbyes, leaving for our respective rooms.

"See you, buddy," Anuj called out as he climbed the stairs to his room, dragging his kit behind him. With a smile, I waved back and made my way to my own room.

Soon after an hour, I got ready and made my way to Prachurjya's room.

"I have been waiting forever," he sulked. "Hope Ritika does not kill us both."

"I will handle her," I said.

"Yeah, right," Prachurjya replied with a smirk.

I dialled her number, and the three of us set out for *'The Three Chefs'*, a well-known restaurant on campus.

"Exams are just around the corner," Ritika observed between bites of her meal.

She had ordered French fries and noodles while Prachurjya and I were content with the savoury biryani that the restaurant served.

"Come on, Ritika, don't spoil the mood," Prachurjya protested, equally engaged with his food. Ritika shot a stern look, and Prachurjya decided to focus on his plate.

I contemplated Anuj's words, feeling an adrenaline rush of excitement for the impending cricket match.

"Exams could wait; the impending rivalry couldn't," I thought.

"EAT," Ritika said sharply. "And before you get lost in your thoughts like a hundred times in the past and stare at people, EAT."

"Oh, Ritika," I laughed. "Quite the character, you are."

Her stern gaze shifted between us, and we quickly directed our attention back to our plates.

"What's happening?" Prachurjya said, looking utterly confused.

He had no idea what was going on.

"Nothing that should bother you… Now EAT, BOTH OF YOU," she roared.

Prachurjya and I looked at each other, and at the same time, we said, "Oh, Ritika!"

Soon, laughter filled the air, and we had our food with smiles that failed to fade only until we paid the bill.

"What an incredible trio we have become in such a short time," Prachurjya remarked, clearing his throat.

"Finally, you decide to speak sense," Ritika said.

Prachurjya smirked at her.

I smiled.

"May this trio always remain the same," I wished, and all three of us exchanged smiles.

"Absolute idiots," Ritika labelled us as we made our way back into the university.

Chapter 7

BUTTERFLIES ON THE EVE

On the 19th of February, the day preceding the crucial match, time seemed to slip through my fingers, consumed entirely by thoughts of the impending game. My encounters with Anuj grew scarcer, making me wonder if he, much like me, was tense too. This was Anuj's last chance for redemption and to end the four-year-long drought of a win against the arch-rivals.

I glanced at the notice board of the hostel. It displayed the schedule of the tournament. All the matches that my hostel, *Patkai Men's Hostel*, had to play were highlighted and put up in bold.

'PATKAI MEN'S HOSTEL vs NILACHAL MEN'S HOSTEL - 20th February,' it read.

"What if we fall short tomorrow? What if Anuj's wish remains unfulfilled?"

These questions haunted my mind. I yearned for a win, not just for our hostel but for Anuj, who, for all I knew, deserved this victory after having waited an eternity.

Something about Anuj's words at the juice shop ignited a fervour within me, a burning desire to triumph against *Nilachal Men's Hostel.*

While I was lost in my thoughts, a voice suddenly pulled me back to reality. I recognised it instantly as Anuj's.

"I see you have been lost in thought for quite some time," he said, with a reassuring smile on his face. He rested his hand on my shoulder.

"Don't worry," he said. "Tomorrow will go well."

"I hope," I said and smiled.

Even though he seemed calm, something gave away that he was anxious too.

"Rest well," he added. "See you at the team meeting after dinner."

As he patted my shoulder, a special bond seemed to deepen between us. Anuj felt more like an older brother than a senior; his calm and composed demeanour often brought a sense of tranquillity to me.

That night, after we had completed our dinner, we gathered in the common room for one final meeting before the match. Anuj addressed the team, boosting their spirits.

"Excited, team?" he asked.

He got up from the chair he was sitting on. He then stood facing us, and the rest of the team was standing in a semicircle, waiting eagerly to hear from him.

"I know you are all a little excited and a little tense," he continued, "But remember, the course of the match is in your hands.

"You and only you can help yourself."

"You are already better than most to have reached here, so why worry?"

Suddenly, the anxiety in the team diminished as enthusiasm soared.

With every sentence Anuj completed, the cheers grew louder, and the claps thundered.

He stressed that the collective effort of all fifteen team members, on and off the field, was what mattered most—underlining the essence of teamwork.

He reminded us not to be swayed by the opposition's crowd, even if they taunted and jeered.

With his motivating words, he instilled confidence in all of us first-year players, including me. He emphasized that if we believed in our abilities and gave our best effort, nothing could stand in the way of our victory.

Afterward, the team spent another hour discussing tactics, strategies, and technicalities. I had hoped for a personal word from Anuj, but it never came, leaving me feeling a bit disappointed.

"Ensure you rest properly," he advised before we dispersed to our rooms.

As I made my way to my room, I heard Anuj finally call my name.

I turned to face him, and he simply smiled.

"You are going to do great tomorrow," he said.

His words lifted my spirits.

"So will you," I replied before heading to my room.

"Good luck, Madhav," I whispered to myself, my mind brimming with excitement.

But as I lay in bed, sleep eluded me. My mind raced with thoughts of the upcoming match, imagining countless scenarios: hitting the winning runs, taking the first wicket, or pulling off a spectacular catch.

"You and only you can help yourself," Anuj's words echoed in my mind, making rest impossible. As I lay there, my phone vibrated, but I was too lost in thoughts of the next day's match to check it. An hour later, when I finally decided to call it a night, I picked up my phone for one last look. The notification that greeted me made my eyes light up.

My hands almost trembled, and my heart dropped for a second.

'Kuhi Sharma has accepted your friend request,' the screen read.

"Yes! Yes! Yes!" I exclaimed, elated.

I could not believe my eyes. It felt wonderful, better than I had felt in a very long time.

I had almost given up on the hope of her accepting the request; after all, it had been days since I had sent it.

But she did, perhaps just at the right time.

"She is amazing," I whispered to myself as I was finally able to scroll through the entire profile.

"Anuj, you were right. Tomorrow is our day; in fact, my day has just begun."

With these thoughts swirling in my mind, I finally found peace. I closed my eyes, letting the weight of the day slip away, and drifted into a restful slumber.

I was ready for the challenges of the next day, relieved that my lingering anxieties had been put to rest.

Chapter 8

TWO IN TWO

The blaring alarm on my phone shattered the morning's silence, waking me from a restless, less than four-hour sleep. Glancing at the clock, I realised we had just over an hour left before we took the field. In a rush, I bolted from my bed, hastily readied myself, and slung my cricket kit over my shoulder before heading to Anuj's room.

Anuj was almost ready by the time I arrived, lacing up his shoes. He greeted me with an encouraging smile.

"Ready, champ?" he asked while attending to the other shoe.

"I am ready, I think," I stammered, my heart racing.

He smiled but did not say anything in return.

With our kits in tow, we set off to join the rest of the team in the common room. As we entered, I spotted Jayanta running through his drills, while Bhaskar playfully mimicked him. The room buzzed with nervous energy, but everyone was putting on a brave face.

Upon arrival, Anuj gave a reassuring pep talk, something we all desperately needed.

"Jayanta, you will open the innings with Jyotish today. Remember, a good start is crucial. Kushal, Hajong, and I will form the middle order. If we lose early wickets, we will need an anchor."

Tensions were palpable, but the team's determination was unwavering.

"I have already said what is needed; all of you know your roles; it is time for some action," he concluded.

"Give your best, guys."

He then formally announced the playing eleven, and once the team was announced, we made our way to the ground.

"Madhav, it is your job to make sure we don't falter in the death overs," Anuj reminded me as we took the shortcut to the ground, crossing the football field.

I nodded, my anxiety mingling with determination.

I took a few deep breaths to compose myself.

The air was charged with anticipation as we gathered for a final huddle.

"Alright, time for the toss," Anuj declared. "Good luck, one last time."

He ventured to the pitch with the rival captain for the toss. Moments later, we found ourselves on the field with the ball in my hand for the first over. Everything was happening so quickly that I had barely any time to process anything.

We lost the toss and were sent to bowl first.

"Remember, do what you always do," Anuj told me as he took his position behind the stumps next to the keeper.

The crowd's roars faded into the background as I focused on the batsman and the wicket. I marked my run-up and steadied myself for the task. A good start was imperative.

"Focus," I whispered to myself.

I was steaming in and could no longer see or hear anything other than the batsman and the pitch.

I released the ball, and the batsman swung for a massive hit as if to smash it out of the park on the very first ball. Thankfully, the ball nicked his edge, sending it soaring upwards. Anuj was under it, and he made no mistake; he took a clean catch, dismissing the opposition captain on the very first ball. A wave of exhilaration washed over me as I ran towards Anuj. I was on cloud nine. He congratulated me, and the team joined in.

I had picked up a wicket off my first ball; the sentiments were running high; I could not have asked for anything more to start off with.

I could see Prachurjya dancing in the crowd in delight, and I raised my arm towards him as if to thank him for his support. He beamed at me and started dancing even more enthusiastically.

As the match went on, we proceeded to dismantle their innings over the next two hours, keeping them to a modest total of a hundred and twenty runs. I managed to take three wickets in my four overs, and Bhaskar and Uttam chipped in with two each.

It was then our turn to bat. As we began, the openers provided a strong start. Jayanta and Jyotish set the tone until Jayanta got out, having contributed significantly to the score. At forty-six for the loss of one wicket in six overs, we needed less than a run per ball to win.

Anuj entered the fray, playing some remarkable strokes. After sixteen overs, we were at ninety-six for three, requiring twenty-five runs from four overs. The stage was set for a historic win; our camp was elated. Nothing could have possibly gone wrong from there on; there was no way we could bottle from that position. But what happened next left a lot of mouths ajar. In one disastrous over, the opposition managed to run Kushal and then Sidharth out. I stepped up to bat, my heart pounding.

"We have to finish this from here," Anuj said, his voice calm. "It is as easy as it gets."

With renewed confidence from Anuj's words, we played out the next two overs carefully, scoring only five runs but, crucially, not losing any more wickets.

With two overs to go, we needed twenty more runs. The game hung in the balance.

Anuj was on strike, and we managed to run hard enough to get two crucial runs from the first delivery itself. Anuj then scored a boundary off the third ball of the over.

"Good shot," I said. "Another boundary and the pressure would be on them."

Anuj smiled and went back.

Anuj was batting well, and it looked like he would be the one to guide us home, but in the next ball, the bowler gave the ball a bit of flight, and Anuj stepped out of his wicket but failed to connect.

The collective gasp from our team and supporters was loud enough for me to hear from the other end of the wicket.

He turned back but was stumped well short of his crease. He was out, and my heart sank. The section of the crowd rooting for us went silent, and the opposition celebrated as if they had taken the final wicket.

Anuj was looking miserable; he was cursing himself for having done that.

"I shouldn't have done that," he said.

As he was walking back, he punched my glove and said, "Madhav, see us through; I know you will do it."

I nodded at him.

He tapped me on the shoulder before walking away.

Uttam came in to bat next, and he was looking petrified.

"Alright! Listen, do all you can but do not throw your wicket," I said. "We can win this from here if we stay till the end. Focus!"

He took his stance, and the bowler came in to bowl the penultimate delivery of that over.

Uttam managed to tap the ball, but there was no run.

The next ball, he swung his bat with all his might. The ball took the inside edge of the bat, slipped between the keeper's legs, and we managed to collect two runs.

"Lucky!" I said, and we both smiled.

"Alright, twelve off six; gettable… let us try our best."

He gave me a nod and punched my glove.

It was my turn to face the last over, and I had only managed to score one run off three balls until then. Without Anuj at the other end, it was make or break for me and the team, and anxiety started to build.

"We can't lose it from here," I reminded myself. "Focus."

The crowd tensely watched as I took my stance, and the bowler ran in. The first ball narrowly missed the top of my off stump, causing collective gasps from the audience even louder than the delivery that stumped Anuj.

"Focus," I shouted internally.

Twelve off five, it was getting tougher with each passing ball. However, the next ball was going to be different.

The bowler ran in to deliver the next ball, and I sensed immediately that it was in my hitting zone. I swung hard, and the ball sailed over the straight boundary, securing a crucial six. The crowd erupted in cheers, and my teammates celebrated. Anuj, however, signalled me to stay put.

We needed six runs from four balls, and the next delivery offered another opportunity. If I missed, it would have meant game over for us and the end of Anuj's dreams, but if I connected, it would mean everything to us.

Not contemplating much, I swung again, connecting perfectly. The ball sailed over the mid-wicket boundary, and with those two hits, we had won the match. Victory was ours. Our hostel supporters roared with delight as the opposition fell into silence. My teammates rushed to hug me. Anuj looked ecstatic.

"I knew you would do it," he exclaimed, patting me on the back.

"But you did give me a heart attack with these shots," he said as he lifted my hand in the air. We had defeated *Nilachal Men's Hostel* for the first time in four years.

Prachurjya and Ritika joined us, offering their congratulations. Prachurjya was ecstatic and gave me a bear hug.

"Drenched in sweat," he said and regretted instantly.

"What else do you expect?" Ritika said, clearly surprised at Prachurjya's ability to not notice the obvious.

Ritika playfully teased, "You stink, by the way."

We laughed, and the camaraderie was evident. "What's friendship without a little sweat?" I quipped, chasing Ritika as she protested.

"Stay away," she shouted, trying to escape my hug, but she failed.

We joined together, a triumphant trio, celebrating the well-deserved victory.

"Good job, Mr. Cricketer," Ritika finally said.

"Thanks. Do I still stink?" I chuckled.

"Yes!" both Prachurjya and Ritika said in unison.

"Right," I said and wrapped my arms around them.

"*Eww*," they said, teasingly jumping away.

Chapter 9

THE FIRST TEXT

The hostel was buzzing with excitement after our long-awaited victory over our arch-rivals. For the first time in four years, we had bested them, and the celebrations within the hostel were nothing short of euphoric.

Outside the hostel entrance, Rohit, a third-year senior, greeted me with commendations.

"Madhav, you were absolutely brilliant today."

Piyush, a final-year student, beamed with enthusiasm.

"What a game, what a result."

A large placard on the notice board offered congratulations to the team, reading: *"Bravo! PATKAI MEN'S HOSTEL, Bravo!"*

Inside the hostel, I was showered with congratulations from at least fifty fellow boarders, making me utter more *'thank-yous'* than I had in my entire life. Once the celebrations and the post-match meeting died down, we left for our respective rooms. After placing my cricket kit bag under my bed, I cleared the pile of clothes that had been sitting on my chair. I sat down and took a moment to reflect on the events of the day.

From the start of the match to my very first delivery, Anuj's surprising dismissal, and my winning hit, it was a day that I could not have asked more from.

Exhausted, I nearly drifted off to sleep on the chair when Prachurjya stormed into my room, almost tumbling me off the chair.

"I thought you would be ready by now," he said, appearing slightly displeased. "Hurry up, please."

"You had promised to go out for lunch if we won."

"Can we do it tomorrow?" I asked, drained from the day's excitement.

"It is already four-thirty anyway… I am too tired."

"No," he protested, pulling my arm.

Too tired to resist, I begrudgingly rose, took a shower, and prepared to leave for lunch. As we headed to the restaurant, Prachurjya recounted, for the umpteenth time, how everyone had applauded the team's performance.

"When Anuj got out, I was sure we were going to lose the match," he said.

"Yeah, but it wasn't to be," I replied.

"Because of you," he beamed.

"Who else?" I joked.

Just then, my phone buzzed, but I was too hungry and tired to check it. After we finished our meal, I paid the bill, and we returned to the hostel.

"Wanna take a detour?" Prachurjya asked.

"Not even for a million dollars," I replied.

"Fine," he sulked.

Ten minutes later, we reached the hostel, and Prachurjya headed to his room. I trudged to my room, struggling with each step up the stairs.

Just as I was about to change and give in to the fatigue, I heard a knock on my door. I was annoyed, not in the mood to hear more about the match. Reluctantly, I opened the door, but to my surprise, it was Ashish, the same person I had met in Prachurjya's room the other day.

"Mind if I come in?" he asked eerily.

"May I?" he added.

"Oh, sorry, I mean, yes, why not," I fumbled.

"Thanks," he said, sitting on my bed. Ashish looked curious, his gaze darting around my room.

"Nice room you have!" he commented, studying everything like a curious child.

"Thanks," I said.

"Did you have lunch?" he asked after a pause.

"Oh yes," I replied. "Prachurjya and I went out."

"That's nice. I could have joined you too," he said, looking slightly displeased.

"Next time, we shall all go together," I said awkwardly.

"Next time it will be," he beamed.

Ashish had a habit of fidgeting with things and moving them from their original position. He had opened and closed the lid of my laptop, flipped my phone on the bed, and glanced through some books on my table. I was starting to get a bit annoyed and hoped he would leave soon.

"Is there anything I can help you with though?" I asked, impatient.

His eccentric nature was putting me off, and I could not wait for him to leave so that I could have my much-needed sleep.

"Oh no, I was just admiring your things," he said with an awkward grin.

"Things?" I asked curiously.

He only nodded his head.

"I'll change into more comfortable clothing. Give me a minute," I said.

"Sure," he replied.

He then began humming a strange tune I did not recognise, turned a few pages of my half-read book, and began playing with my pen on the table.

But as I had changed, Ashish got up abruptly and began to leave the room.

"Congratulations on the win," he said as he left.

"Thanks," I replied, still bewildered.

After he left, I shook my head in confusion and closed the door. I was too tired to reflect on it.

"Strange guy," I muttered.

Fatigue from the intense match caused me to fall onto my bed, and I closed my eyes, drifting into sleep.

It felt like the most peaceful sleep ever.

However, I was rudely awakened by a loud banging on my door.

"Not again," I said and got up.

Rubbing my eyes, I opened the door. Prachurjya was standing there, looking agitated.

"What now?" I asked, squinting.

"What now?" he exclaimed. "I have been calling you for four hours. You didn't answer your phone, and you missed dinner. I genuinely, for once, entertained the idea of you being dead."

"Who sleeps like that?"

I checked my phone and saw nine missed calls. It was half past eleven, and it was too late to have dinner. I couldn't believe I had slept for so long.

"But why didn't I hear my phone ring?" I wondered.

Surprisingly, I discovered that my phone had been set to silent mode.

"Very unusual," I admitted.

"If you sleep like a donkey and snore like a pig, how do you expect to hear anything?" Prachurjya teased.

I decided to ignore his comment.

I was still confused, and then suddenly, something struck me, and my eyes that looked squinted moments back seemed wide open.

"Do you have Ashish's number?" I asked.

"Why?" Prachurjya inquired.

"Do you have it or not?" I asked.

"I don't, but Biswajyoti might," he replied.

I called Biswajyoti, who provided me with Ashish's number.

His phone rang, and he picked up after what seemed like a lifetime.

"Ashish, did you put my phone on silent?" I asked him.

"What?" he responded timidly.

"Did you put my phone on silent mode?" I repeated.

"I might have. I was just checking if it works," he replied lazily.

"Why would you do that?" I asked.

"I was just checking," he replied, unfazed.

I disconnected the call and mumbled to myself.

Prachurjya, who had no idea what had transpired, looked at me.

"What was that all about?" he asked.

"Do you have any food?" I inquired.

"In my room," he said.

"Great, I'll tell you everything, but let's have some food first. I can't go back to bed to only wake up in the middle of the night feeling hungry," I said.

"As if it isn't already midnight," he sulked.

"Sleep for hours, miss dinner, and then come to me."

I shot him a disgusted look and headed straight to his room. After finishing the snacks, I explained the story of Ashish's sudden exit to both Prachurjya and Biswajyoti.

"Biswajyoti's friend, that one," Prachurjya said at the end of the tale.

Biswajyoti shot him a fierce look and retorted, "You introduced me to him."

"What?" I said, bewildered.

"He is joking," Prachurjya said, clearing his throat.

"No, no," Biswajyoti said. "Don't you know they are school buddies?"

I looked at Prachurjya with a very surprising look on my face.

"Well, we were not buddies," Prachurjya clarified.

"We went to the same school, and when paths crossed here once again, I introduced him to Biswajyoti."

"In all this time, you never mentioned it?" I asked, appalled.

"You never asked," Prachurjya replied. "And I did not think it was that important."

"He has always been this way though, ever since I have known him," Biswajyoti added.

"Why is he like that?" I inquired.

"Oh, come on," Prachurjya said. "Don't judge him. He may be a little odd at times, but he is a nice person."

"Clearly," I retorted. "Anyway, I should probably get going."

"Yes please," Prachurjya said.

"You have completed your quota; let us complete ours."

"Ours… I see," I laughed.

"Go away," Prachurjya smirked and shut the door.

Though I had satisfied my hunger, I knew I could not go back to sleep since I had already slept for hours. I made my way back to my room, where I sat down on my bed and unlocked my phone. This was the first time after the match that I had the chance or the will to check my phone.

Pulling down the notification tab, I scrolled through the messages on my social media application. As I did, my eyes widened, and my jaw dropped in amazement. There was a text message.

It was from her, the first time she had messaged me.

"Congratulations on the win, Madhav… was there on the field," the message read.

My happiness knew no bounds. I stared at that line, my eyes locked on the screen, refusing to look away. Winning the match seemed insignificant compared to this moment. She had messaged me earlier in the day, and I had missed it.

Gathering my composure, I began typing a response.

"Hey, thank you sooooooo much. It means a lot, realllllly. Thank you so, so much."

But then I reconsidered and opted for brevity.

"Hey, thank you so much," I wrote instead.

After much contemplation, I clicked on the *'send'* icon and took a deep breath. I waited for another two hours, eagerly checking my phone, but there was no reply. She was however offline.

"She must have gone to bed," I thought, still smiling from what had transpired.

I turned off the light and read the message she had sent once more.

"Congratulations on the win, Madhav… was there on the field."

"She saw me win it for my team. She knows I did it, and most importantly, she knows my name," I said aloud, overwhelmed with joy. I closed my eyes, feeling the happiest, and drifted into dreams filled with happiness.

Chapter 10

MAYBE

I woke up early the next day, having slept through most of the previous day after the match. As I checked my phone, it read six o'clock. Outside, the birds were chirping and greeted the day with cheerful melodies. The windows were covered in a thin layer of morning mist, and the atmosphere felt unusually serene, a stark contrast to the usual morning rush.

I rose from my bed and felt the brisk winter morning air gently brushing my cheeks when I stepped outside my room. However, I decided against venturing further and returned to my room. Sitting on the edge of my bed, I reminisced about the previous night. I wanted to read her text message again. Despite having read it countless times, each read was as thrilling as the first.

"Congratulations on the win, Madhav… was there on the field."

I stared at the message for minutes.

"Life is good," I said to myself.

Whether it was the early morning energy or the fact that she had sent me the first text, I felt the need to express my emotions, to tell someone what it felt like. However, this was something I could not tell anyone, so I came up with an idea. Writing was a passion I had cultivated over the years, especially in moments of great joy or profound sadness. I decided that it was the perfect time to pen down my feelings.

Rummaging through my cluttered cupboard, I eventually located my old diary, a cherished possession, unfortunately covered in dust. As I flipped through the pages, I rediscovered a treasure trove of memories from my school and college days. This diary had been my confidant for years, known only to my mother.

Just as I was about to put pen to paper, my phone rang.

It was Ritika, and I wondered what made her call so unusually early.

"Hello?" I answered.

"Mr. Cricketer, what got you up so early today?" Ritika inquired.

I was surprised.

"Did you have a prophetic dream or something?" I teased.

"You are an idiot. I just noticed you were online." she said.

"Are you stalking me?" I joked.

"You wish," she replied.

"Anyway, listen, I called to let you know that since today is Sunday, we are going to the movies. Also, make sure to tell Prachurjya not to bail."

"When did we make this plan?" I asked.

"We did not. I did... this morning. We are meeting at eleven o'clock sharp near the gate."

"It definitely doesn't sound like you are asking, but okay," I sighed.

Obviously, I could not say no, even if I wanted to.

"Alright, Ritika. See you at eleven o'clock sharp." I finally gave in.

Before I could say anything else, she hung up the phone. I wasn't sure about going to the movies, but I had no intention of angering Ritika by declining her proposal.

I shook my head and smiled.

"It indeed is a good day."

Returning to my diary, I started to write. When the clock read half-past eight, I finally put the pen down. I had poured my heart out in the most spontaneous manner I could, without revisiting my words.

Those eyes had something about them. No, they were not blue, neither were they like the ones they tell you about in movies, but there was something in those eyes that set her apart. Her eyes glowed like the bright stars of a clear night sky. They were bright and twinkling, and if I could, I would never stop staring at them. She had eyes which resembled a black hole; the moment you looked at them, there was no returning back. They say, "Behind the most beautiful eyes lie secrets deeper than the most mysterious waters." Those eyes most certainly made me want to dive into them and never resurface again. But it was not just the eyes she had.

Her voice was a melodious symphony that could halt time. It felt as though her euphonious tone reverberated in all directions. It is not every day that I get to hear her speak, but if I could, her voice is the only thing I would want to listen to for the rest of my life. She does not need to do special things to look special because she is 'special, in her own beautiful way' and I realised this the moment I gazed into those very special eyes of hers.

Maybe I have fallen for her to the point of no return. Maybe she has left me captivated in a way that can never be repeated. Even the tiniest sight of her makes my heart judder. It is like an engine out of control. She makes me want to live life in a way that can only be experienced and never described. I was not acquainted with this dimension of life until she showed me the way. She and I aren't together, and there is a good chance we never will be. There is a common saying, "There are things that can never be yours, no matter how much you try or whatever you do." Maybe it will work out someday, maybe not; but then 'maybe' is probably the most polarising expression this world has ever heard of. 'Maybe' can keep you moving or stop you altogether; it can motivate you or demoralise you, it can help you put your best foot forward or might make you retrace your steps, it can even push you to give it your all, or it can take away your everything. But sometimes, despite its negativities, a 'maybe' becomes a beacon of hope because somewhere deep down, the heart knows "Kuhi, maybe it will work out someday."

I checked my phone, but Kuhi was still not online. I smiled and got ready, then called Prachurjya to inform him of Ritika's plan. By ten forty-five, we had both reached the gate, waiting for Ritika. A few minutes later, she appeared in the distance.

"She asks us to be on time and arrives late herself," Prachurjya grumbled.

"Try telling that to her," I laughed.

Just then, my phone beeped. For some reason, I knew this had to be the message I was waiting for; this had to be from Kuhi.

My heart raced in anticipation; I could not wait to open the text, but I had to wait for that. I was surrounded by a lot of people, and I couldn't risk Prachurjya or Ritika finding out about it.

"Glad you made it in time," Ritika said as she arrived.

"Look who is talking about being on time," Prachurjya shot back.

"Excuse me?" Ritika replied, her tone fierce.

Prachurjya pretended to clear his throat dramatically.

"What's so amusing, Mr. *I-can-hit-two-sixes-in-two-balls*?" she said.

"Why are you glowing so much today and what is that with the unusual smile?"

"You are crazy," I said, unable to suppress my smile.

"Weirdo," she retorted, glancing away.

"Kuhi, you are beautiful," I whispered to myself, smiling as I waved at the bus approaching us.

I could hardly wait to board the bus and respond to the text, which I believed was from Kuhi. With each passing moment, I was falling deeper for her without even realising it.

Chapter 11

THE OPEN SECRET

The bus arrived seconds later. However, it was overcrowded with people who were almost at war with one another to get a seat. It was jam-packed, and we couldn't find seats for ourselves. Being a holiday, the bus was so full that there was hardly any room for us to even breathe, let alone move. It was a bright sunny day, and the lack of space in the bus made me extremely uncomfortable, causing me to sweat profusely.

"Let's just get off," Prachurjya suggested while wiping sweat from his forehead.

"Yes, please," I said, equally annoyed.

"I knew it was a bad idea."

Prachurjya nodded vigorously.

"What?" interjected Ritika.

"Nothing," we both said.

She shook her head and looked away. She was checking her phone, and I considered her extremely lucky for being able to do it, as I was unable to even move my neck, being sandwiched between half a dozen people from all sides.

"Hey, why don't you take this seat?" a boy seated right next to where Ritika stood suddenly said.

"I do not mind standing…"

Ritika turned to him, her expression one of surprise.

"Excuse me?" she said.

"No… I mean… I thought you might want to have a seat," he corrected.

"I shall be getting down soon, so I thought, you know…"

"Oh no, no… I am with my friends," she said, looking slightly embarrassed.

Prachurjya's eyes lit up as he instantly knew this was his moment to tease Ritika.

"Chivalry is not very common these days, is it?" Prachurjya said to me while looking up.

He was trying very hard not to burst into laughter, and so was I.

"Shut up, Prachurjya," she squealed, her cheeks turning pink as she tried to act unaffected.

I grinned at her, and she raised her eyebrows as if to say, "*Please stop making this awkward.*"

"Thank you so much," she finally said to the boy. "But we are getting down soon too."

"Well, okay… If you say so," he said and got off the bus at the next stop.

As other people got down, we finally managed to find seats for ourselves. I sat between the two of them.

"Can you smell something in the air?" Prachurjya asked.

Both Ritika and I looked at him with confusion.

"Love, idiots, love," he announced dramatically.

I could not hold it anymore, and I laughed out loud.

"Idiots, both of you," Ritika shot back, rolling her eyes.

"Right!" both Prachurjya and I said in unison.

We noticed several eyes on us, bewildered at our cheerful demeanour amidst the sweat.

We got off at the next stop, and I was relieved.

"I would have evaporated if I spent another minute on that bus," I said, glancing at my soaked T-shirt.

"I am sure Ritika wouldn't mind another hour," Prachurjya cackled.

I bit my lip to stifle my smile.

"If you laugh this time, I'll strangle you, Madhav," she threatened.

"I understand the threatening. Now that you have backup, you won't have to worry about finding a seat in a crowded bus ever again," Prachurjya teased.

I pretended to turn around, concealing my laughter.

"Stop now," she grimaced. "Besides, he was being a gentleman, unlike the two of you."

Prachurjya and I exchanged mischievous glances, nodding exaggeratedly.

"If you both are done, can we please enter the theatre?" she said.

"Yes, why not?" we replied, beaming at her.

"Idiots, both of you," she muttered again.

"She scolds me more than my teacher did during school," Prachurjya quipped.

"No wonder you turned out like this," Ritika shot back coldly.

I chuckled, but Prachurjya didn't find it funny at all.

We made our way to the theatre, and to my surprise, it was no different from the bus; but at least we had ample space to move around this time.

The usher guided us to our seats. Ritika sat in the middle, and I took the seat to her right.

After a few minutes, the movie began. Ritika looked thrilled, as her favourite actor was featured.

Suddenly, my phone pinged. I had almost forgotten to check it amid the bus chaos.

"Anything wrong?" Ritika asked.

"Of course not," I replied, secretly hoping she didn't have psychic abilities.

As the movie set its pace, I sneaked my hand into my pocket, carefully retrieving my phone.

Unlocking it, I found a text from Kuhi.

"*You are welcome!*" the first message read.

"*Good luck for your next matches,*" the latest one said.

I smiled, pondering the right way to respond while glancing at Ritika to ensure she wasn't watching.

She was engrossed in the movie, barely blinking.

"*Thank you so much once again… I'll try my best,*" I typed.

In less than a minute, another text from her appeared, making me smile even wider.

I turned towards Ritika; her eyes were still glued to the screen.

"*Win the cup xD… At least I'll be able to tell people you are a classmate.*"

I was elated. I felt like dancing but knew it wasn't the best idea.

"*Shouldn't be a problem, now that I have your wishes with me.*" I replied quickly.

Her reply came in under half a minute.

"*Haha… You'll do well xD… Good luck again.*"

"*Thanks, Kuhi ;)*" I replied.

"*:)*" she answered, sending a smiling emoticon.

I locked my phone and put it back into my pocket. This time, however, when I turned to look at Ritika, I found her staring right at me in the eye. My heart raced.

"What?" she asked.

"What?" I echoed.

"We are here for a movie, Madhav. Focus on the big screen, not your phone," she whispered.

Partially relieved that she hadn't seen anything, I shrugged it off.

Once the movie ended, we had lunch together before boarding the six o'clock bus back to the university.

Ritika and I sat together, while Prachurjya took a seat one row ahead.

"Madhav," Prachurjya said nonchalantly.

"Yes?" I replied.

"Chivalry isn't very common," he repeated.

I giggled, but this time Ritika smiled too, in a very cunning way. The moment our eyes met; my laughter halted.

I felt a strange certainty that she was up to something.

"Why did you stop? Please continue, Madhav… Why don't you just '*Ku-HEE-HEE*'?"

"What?" I asked sheepishly.

"Just what you heard," she said coolly.

"Not what you think," I stammered, trying to maintain my composure.

"That's what I saw," Ritika replied.

"Just a friend," I whispered.

"I said nothing," she sneered.

"Prachurjya," she said, "You were right… Love is indeed 'in the air.'"

"Eh, what?" Prachurjya asked, looking bewildered.

"Love is in the air," she scoffed.

I silently pleaded for her to be quiet. But who could stop Ritika once she was unleashed?

"*Ku-hee-hee-hee*," she continued relentlessly until we reached our destination.

Chapter 12

LIKING FOR THE LIBRARY

"Hey," Ritika whispered in the middle of class, tapping my wrist.

"What?" I said without looking at her.

"Nothing," she said, a mischievous glint in her eyes.

"Madhav," she called out again a minute later.

"What?" I snapped, my irritation rising.

The professor shot me a piercing look instantly. I pretended to concentrate on the book, glancing down quickly.

"Ritika! What's wrong?" I mumbled, feeling the tension precarious.

"*Hee-hee-hee*," she hooted.

I shot her a disgusted look, shaking my head in disappointment.

"I cannot believe I am saying this, but Ritika, you will get us thrown out of class," I whispered.

"Also, you are imagining things anyway."

"Yeah right," she retorted, her tone dripping with sarcasm.

As our classes ended, I felt my patience wearing thin with her incessant "*Hee-hee-hee.*"

It had become a relentless echo in my mind.

"Does she know about it?" she asked as we walked back to our hostels together after class.

We often strolled together. However, Prachurjya, being who he was, would often skip the last class before recess. So, Ritika and I usually took the long walk from the department to our hostels.

My hostel was, however, a few hundred metres away from Ritika's, so I would first accompany her and then walk towards mine.

"Who knows about what?" I asked, feigning ignorance.

"Come on, Madhav… I saw that look on your face at the cinema hall," she said, her tone turning serious.

"It was written all over your face."

I stared at her for a moment, not to intimidate her, but because I knew she was right, and I had nothing to prove her otherwise.

"You are only imagining things," I finally said. "Besides, it was so dark in there; one could hardly see anything, let alone the 'look' on my face."

"No point in lying to me, Mr. Cricketer. Try this with Prachurjya!" she snapped, her eyes narrowing.

"Prachurjya is not as gullible as you think," I said, forcing a smile.

"Surely not as much as you think me to be," she said coolly.

"Anyway, you do know that we have exams in three weeks, right?"

She raised an eyebrow, a hint of concern creeping into her voice.

"I know," I said, looking grim.

"I haven't even opened my books once."

"I know," she said, clicking her tongue sympathetically.

"Of course, you have been keeping yourself very busy, haven't you?" A hint of sarcasm danced in her words.

I chose to ignore that.

"This evening, join me in the library, and I might be able to help," she said.

"Library?" I asked. "Are you sure?"

"Of course... Besides, if you are lucky, you might be in for a treat," she winked playfully as she turned left towards the alley leading to her hostel.

"Treat?" I asked, intrigued as she entered the gate.

"See you in the evening; you will get to know," she said, waving goodbye.

I sighed and walked towards my hostel.

Soon after the sun had set that evening, I spotted Ritika waiting outside my hostel at exactly half-past six. She had a few books and a notebook in one hand, while the other clutched a transparent box filled with an assortment of pens, highlighters, and pencils.

"You are a walking-talking stationery shop," I laughed, pulling her leg.

"Idiot," she shot back.

"Come on, let's go!" she urged, her excitement palpable as we made our way to the library.

Entering the library for the first time was overwhelming. The three-storey building loomed before me, painted pristine white with a grand porcelain sign at the entrance. Inside, the vast expanse housed more rooms than I could count, and three reading halls nearly the size of banquet halls. Just inside the entrance, a security guard sat at a desk, keeping a register of everyone who visited.

"Never been here before, have you?" Ritika teased as I gazed around in awe.

I shook my head, biting my lip in embarrassment.

"No wonder," she said, her disappointment barely concealed. "Now, follow me and remember: no talking; it's a library, after all."

"Ritika," I replied, perplexed, "I know that."

"We shall see," she said, leading me to the third floor.

We entered a grand hall filled with focused readers. I scanned the room and spotted two empty chairs tucked in a quiet corner.

"One last thing: no fiddling with phones until we are done," she commanded.

Before I could respond, she flipped open her book, already immersed in her study.

"What a mess," I mumbled under my breath, five minutes after staring at the notes.

"*Shhhh!* Keep that voice down," she whispered urgently.

I nodded vigorously, and she flashed me a smile that was both encouraging and mischievous.

For the next two hours, however, she transformed into an excellent tutor, helping me cover everything I needed to grasp for the upcoming exams. With her guidance, concepts that had seemed daunting became clear. I felt a newfound confidence blossoming; my exams might not be a disaster after all.

"Alright, let's take a break," she announced after our productive study session. "We can afford some leisure."

After twenty minutes of downtime at the canteen, during which she finished off at least three cups of coffee, a handful of muffins, and an entire packet of wafers—she returned to our study space.

"I don't even think I'll be able to have dinner tonight," she said, munching on the last piece of wafer.

"I am sure," I replied, astonished by how quickly she ate everything.

"They should really conduct research on you; a body isn't supposed to consume like that," I said.

She shot me a fierce look, and I quickly shifted my gaze, pretending to look away.

Once settled back into our seats, we resumed studying. About ten minutes later, Ritika paused, her eyes sparkling with excitement.

"Remember I told you that you might get lucky?"

"Eh… yes?" I replied, bewildered.

"In the afternoon, you mean?"

"Yes," she chimed, leaning closer.

"You just got lucky."

She pointed toward the entrance of the hall.

Confused, I followed her gaze, and my eyes widened as I saw Kuhi walking in. My heart raced, a broad smile breaking across my face.

"Easy now, Mr. Cricketer," Ritika giggled. "Don't make it too obvious."

"Ritika," I almost exclaimed before she shot me a sharp look, reminding me we were in a library.

"Tell me again, was I really imagining things?" she asked, her voice dropping to a whisper.

I remained silent, realising she was sharper than I had given her credit for.

"Alright, shall we get back to studying?" she suggested after a moment.

"Yes," I replied, still smiling uncontrollably.

"Stop smiling, Madhav," she scolded playfully, slapping my wrist with her pen.

I couldn't help it; I wasn't expecting Kuhi to be there, and my lips seemed to have a mind of their own. I tried to refocus on Ritika, who was nudging me gently to regain my attention.

"Madhav, do you want to pass or not?" she scoffed, exasperated.

Realising she was right, I nodded at her with a grin.

"Let's resume, then?" she asked.

"Of course," I replied cheerfully. "For as long as you want."

We studied for a few more hours until it was nearly ten, and the library had emptied significantly.

"Does she come here every day?" I asked Ritika as we made our way out.

"Do you mean *Kuuu-Heee-Heee?*" she asked, a teasing edge in her voice.

I flushed, slightly embarrassed.

"Very often" she replied coolly.

"Cool," I said, trying to play it off.

"Tomorrow, same time?" Ritika asked, her expression brightening.

"Every day at the same time," I winked, with a wide grin on my face.

Chapter 13

LUCK OR NO LUCK

The days leading up to the exams passed quickly. We secured victories in our remaining matches, propelling us to the finals, which was scheduled for the week after our exams concluded. Following Ritika's advice, I focused on completing my exam preparations before turning my attention to the crucial final match.

Ritika and I had made it a daily ritual to visit the library, each with our own distinct goals. While Ritika diligently revised the entire syllabus, likely more times than I could count, my main goal was to catch a glimpse of Kuhi. Surprisingly, despite my initial reluctance to study, Ritika managed to guide me through the syllabus. To my amazement, I felt more prepared and confident for the exams than I had expected.

"I am screwed tomorrow," Prachurjya exclaimed in a panic. It was the eve of our first exam, and I joined Prachurjya, Biswajyoti, and Ashish in Prachurjya's room.

"I did ask you to come along to the library, didn't I?" I reminded him.

"Yes, but…" Prachurjya mumbled.

"But what?" I smirked.

"Nothing…" he said grimly.

I shook my head in exasperation.

Meanwhile, Biswajyoti was fully focused on the study material, trying to memorise a challenging part of a problem that none of us could solve.

"Better to memorise something than leave it blank," Biswajyoti chuckled.

Ashish, on the other hand, seemed the least bothered about the upcoming exam, scrolling through his phone without a care in the world.

After a few minutes, Prachurjya groaned again.

"Oh God! I am doomed."

"Calm down!" I snapped. "It will be fine."

"Easy for you to say," he shot back.

"What do you mean?" I asked.

"Nothing," he sulked.

"Look," I said, trying to stay calm.

"There is not much you can do now. Just go through the material once and hope you retain some of it."

Prachurjya sighed deeply. "Maybe the only thing that can save me now is sheer dumb luck."

'Luck,' a term humans rely on when they feel powerless. If Prachurjya had joined us in the library, he wouldn't have had to depend so much on luck. But sometimes, even getting lucky requires luck. I realised this on the day of our first exam when Prachurjya ended up having his seat allotted just behind Ritika, while I was miles away from them both.

The grin on Prachurjya's face was a sight for everyone to see.

"How did it go?" I asked Prachurjya after the exam.

"Brilliant," he grinned.

"Right," I sighed.

"You do realise this won't happen every time, right?" Ritika commented while reviewing the question paper as we walked out of the department.

"We will see about that," Prachurjya replied confidently, walking ahead.

Ritika shook her head.

Prachurjya could not believe his own luck, and neither could I. From expecting the lowest score in the class, he then seemed certain he would score as high as Ritika.

Prachurjya's earlier words echoed in my mind: "Maybe the only thing that can save me now is sheer dumb luck." He truly lived up to it.

Returning to my room, I collapsed onto my bed—the most comfortable place in a hostel room. I hadn't taken my phone to the exam hall, and upon checking it, I was utterly surprised to see a pending message from Kuhi.

"Hey, good luck for the exams! :)" She had sent it a minute after I had left for the examination hall.

"Hey, thank you! All the best to you too. Sorry for the late reply…" I quickly typed, my heart racing.

I waited for her response; eyes glued to the screen. But it didn't come.

Minutes ticked by, every notification making my heart leap, only for it to be a disappointment. None of them were from Kuhi.

The fact that Kuhi and I were exchanging texts felt surreal. It seemed as if it were only yesterday when I had first seen her, mesmerised in a way I had never experienced before. I smiled, thinking about that day when my phone buzzed again.

It wasn't Kuhi this time either—just Prachurjya asking me to meet him downstairs for lunch. Slightly disappointed, I grabbed my things and headed out to the dining hall.

"How did it go?" Ashish asked as we sat down to eat.

"Not bad. You?" I replied.

"I don't know, but definitely better than Prachurjya," Ashish smirked.

I bit my lip, glancing at Prachurjya, who scoffed.

"What?" Ashish asked.

"Nothing," Prachurjya muttered, pride dripping from his face.

"But you might want to take it back."

Ashish shot him a puzzled look.

Once we finished lunch, we went back to our rooms to prepare for the next exam. Prachurjya, still riding high on his luck, was more relaxed than usual. But luck doesn't always last, and he learned that the hard way the next day when the professor swapped his seat with Biswajyoti, placing him in the front row.

Prachurjya glared at Biswajyoti, as if it were somehow his fault.

"Why me?" Prachurjya groaned after the exam.

"I told you," Ritika said calmly, "luck won't always be on your side."

"Go study for the next exam," she added, walking ahead.

Prachurjya sulked all the way back to the hostel, robbed of his golden opportunity to ace the exams once again. I, however, was eager to check my phone, hoping for a message from Kuhi.

To my delight, a new message had arrived.

"*How did it go?*" she had written.

I couldn't help but grin. She thought about me again.

"*Not too bad,*" I replied quickly. "*Better than I expected, actually. What about you?*"

Her response came almost immediately. "*Better than expected! Though I might have written a random formula on the last question :(What about you? Mastered the art of bluffing yet?*"

I chuckled. Her light-hearted tone made me feel at ease.

"*You wished me luck, so obviously it wouldn't go too bad … ;)*" I typed, a little nervous. I wasn't sure if the playful flirting would work.

But her reply came quickly, easing my nerves.

"Haha! Glad my wishes worked! Good luck for the remaining exams as well..."

I stood there, starting at the screen, smiling like an idiot. I read her message twice, then typed out my response.

"Thank you sooo much, Kuhi!! I hope you do well tomorrow too."

" :) Thanks, Madhav :) and yes, good luck for the final on Sunday..."

I reread her message, savouring the way she used my name and wished me well for the final match. She had a way of brightening my day with just a few words. It felt like the start of something new, something special.

Happiness, I realised, didn't require grand gestures or monumental achievements. Sometimes, it was found in the smallest, most unexpected moments. And I was most certainly going through the happiest phase of my life.

Chapter 14

D-DAY

The days leading up to the finals flew by in a whirlwind of excitement and nerves. We had won every match to get there, and then we were in the finals. Anuj, always the expert strategist, spent more time in my room than his own, discussing strategies for the big game.

"Just one more match, and I can finally breathe," he said, exhaling heavily. "This is my last chance to win the cup for my hostel, and I am giving it my everything."

"I know we will do well," I replied, trying to ease the tension. "We just need to stick to what we have been doing."

But there was something else bothering me—the presence of Subhasish, a senior who had been on the sidelines throughout the tournament. Subhasish had always resented how quickly I rose in the team, especially after my first few matches. Despite my performances, he often made salty remarks, and it was clear he wasn't happy with me being in the playing eleven, particularly for a final of this magnitude.

"You better not screw this up," Subhasish muttered as I passed him in the hallway before our team meeting. His eyes were cold, and I could feel his disdain.

"Don't worry, I'll handle it," I replied, trying to stay calm, but his presence had a way of getting under my skin.

Our opponents, *Kanchenjunga Men's Hostel*, had been dominating their group, and the pressure was mounting. With less than twenty-four hours until the final, Anuj called off practice on the final day, wisely deciding we should rest. Throughout the day, the team stuck together.

Jayanta, our top scorer after Anuj, was itching to hit the field, while everyone else seemed quietly determined. I noticed Subhasish hanging around the team more than usual, his presence unsettling.

After our last strategy session, I headed back to my room. It was almost ten o'clock, and I hoped to see a message from Kuhi. Nothing.

"Maybe she is busy," I muttered, trying not to dwell on it as I crawled into bed.

But sleep didn't come easily. Subhasish's words echoed in my mind. I knew how much he wanted to see me fail. This was Anuj's final match for the hostel, and I wanted to win the trophy for him, but for that I needed to prove myself to people like Subhasish first. The weight of it all pressed on my chest. I tossed and turned, unable to shut off my thoughts. Only in the early hours of the morning did I finally drift off into an uneasy sleep.

I was however, jolted awake by the sound of my alarm. D-Day had arrived. This was it—a day that could either define our legacy or shatter our dreams. I quickly got ready, gulping down my breakfast in record time. Just as I was about to grab my kit bag, my phone vibrated. It was a text from Kuhi.

"Good luck! Hope you have a great game."

I smiled, feeling a sudden surge of energy.

"Thanks, Kuhi. I really needed that. Hope to see you there," I replied, feeling lighter.

Downstairs, the hostel lobby buzzed with excitement. Almost everyone was coming to watch the final. The entire team gathered, getting ready to head to the field.

"Alright, let's keep calm and play to our strengths," Anuj said, addressing the team. "No reason to be nervous. Just another game."

Subhasish, standing at the back, rolled his eyes. "Hope no one crumbles under pressure," he said loudly enough for me to hear. I shot him a look, but Anuj's focus on the game ahead kept me from reacting.

The ground buzzed with the roar of eager spectators, their cheers echoing in my ears like a relentless tide. The cheers from both sides filled the air, creating an electric atmosphere. Anuj and the opposing captain walked to the middle for the toss.

"Heads," Anuj called, but the coin landed tails. We were put into bat. Anuj looked slightly disappointed but quickly composed himself.

"Good batting conditions. The sun is out. Let's just play our game." He said while padding up.

Our openers started strong, and we raced to fifty-nine without loss after seven overs. Just as we thought we were motoring ourselves to a solid score, disaster struck. We lost three wickets in the space of two overs, including Anuj, who was caught in the covers.

This was the final time Anuj walked back with a bat in his hand for the hostel. He looked devastated. Our momentum stalled. Losing one more wicket, we limped to sixty-three for the loss of four wickets by the tenth over, and if we lost another wicket, I would have to go in. Subhasish smirked from the sidelines, clearly enjoying the collapse.

When Jayanta got run out at the start of the eleventh over, it was my turn to bat. I walked out to a daunting task. We were sixty-nine for five, and another wicket would likely seal our fate. I managed to survive the rest of the over, but things only got worse. Two more wickets fell quickly, and I found myself at the crease with Bhaskar.

A tight knot formed in my stomach, the gravity of the moment settling in as I walked to the crease, the ground beneath me feeling both solid and shaky at the same time.

Bhaskar walked up to me; panic written all over his face. "What should we do now? Play safe or swing?"

"Wait for my signal," I said, trying to stay calm.

As I prepared to face the next delivery, I could hear Subhasish shouting from the boundary, "Better not mess this up, kid!"

I blocked the taunts from my mind. Bhaskar blocked the next few balls and got a single. I took a deep breath, surveying the field. I knew this was my moment—to either play it safe and crawl to a modest total if at all or take the risk that could turn the game. I glanced toward Anuj in the pavilion. He nodded, as if giving me the green light.

The next ball was in my slot, and I swung hard. It soared over mid-wicket for a towering six. The next delivery, I punched through the leg side for four. I was in the zone. Every ball felt right, and soon, I raced to fifty in just seventeen balls.

By the end of our innings, we had managed to score a hundred and forty-nine runs. I finished unbeaten on sixty-two, my best innings to date. The late onslaught had given us something to defend, and then it was up to our bowlers.

The second innings, however, passed by like a breeze. We bowled out *Kanchenjunga Men's Hostel* for just ninety-five runs. We had done it. We won.

Euphoria swept over us. Anuj rushed towards me, eyes brimming with tears. "We did it," he choked, pulling me into a hug. The celebrations erupted around us. After years of trying, *Patkai Men's Hostel* had finally lifted the cup.

As the celebrations calmed down, I noticed Subhasish leaning against a tree, arms crossed, his face stony.

"Guess you got lucky," he muttered as I passed him.

"Or maybe I am just good," I shot back, the adrenaline giving me confidence. Subhasish gave me a cold look before disappearing into the crowd.

I had silenced him, and I had shown everybody what I could do.

For a moment in time, I felt like I was invincible.

Just as I was about to rejoin the team, I saw Ritika running towards me, with a huge smile on her face. But she wasn't alone. Walking beside her, almost in slow motion, was a face that caught me by surprise. My heart raced as she got closer.

"Congratulations, Mr. Cricketer," Ritika said, grinning. "Kuhi wants to congratulate you."

I was caught off guard. "Hi... Thank you," I stammered.

Kuhi smiled, a beautiful, warm smile that made my chest tighten.

"I told you; you would do well." She said gently.

"Yes... you did," I mumbled, suddenly very aware of how awkward I sounded.

She smiled again and said, "I'll leave you to celebrate with your team. Bye."

I watched as she turned to leave. My mind raced. Should I say something? Should I stop her?

"What are you doing?" Ritika hissed. "Are you just going to let her walk away?"

Before I could second-guess myself, I called out, "Kuhi!"

She paused and turned. "Yes, Madhav?"

In one breath, I said the words that would change my life forever.

"Would you like to go out this evening?"

Her eyes widened in surprise, and I could feel the shock from Ritika and even Prachurjya, who had just arrived.

For a moment, Kuhi said nothing. Then, she nodded, a small smile on her lips.

"Sure," she said softly, before turning and walking away.

I stood there, grinning like an idiot. The joy of winning the cup paled in comparison to the moment that had just unfolded. Kuhi had said yes.

The Girl in White was finally going out with me, and in that moment, everything felt perfect.

ACT II

Chapter 15

THE FIRST DATE

"One surprising thing about being in love is that you start noticing changes in yourself. Love alters your choices and preferences. It influences you, revamps your likes and dislikes. You become bewitched by that one person you can't stop thinking about. Even food you once despised suddenly becomes your favourite because that one person likes it. Sometimes, being in love, being truly in awe of someone is the most life-altering thing you ever experience..."

Those words resonated with me as I sat across from Kuhi, realising how true they had been since our very first date. My heart raced; everything had happened so fast—from winning the cup for my hostel to asking Kuhi out. And now, there she was, sitting right in front of me. I couldn't help but silently thank God for how perfectly everything had fallen into place.

After a few moments of silent admiration, I finally mustered the courage to clear my throat.

"So… Do you like this place?" I asked, nerves evident in my voice.

"Yes," she replied fervently. "I mean, not that I visit it every day, but yes, this place is wonderful."

As she spoke, I couldn't help but gaze into her glinting eyes. Everything felt like a dream—a beautiful dream that I hadn't planned but was grateful for.

We had been sitting in *'The Three Chefs'* for five minutes, and other than me stealing clandestine glances, we had barely exchanged anything else. I started to worry that this date would turn into a complete disaster—although I wasn't even sure if it was a date; I liked to call it that anyway.

"What would you like to have?" the waiter asked, simpering at me in a peculiar manner. *'The Three Chefs'* was a restaurant I visited frequently, mostly with Ritika. I wondered if seeing me with another girl made the waiter smile strangely at me.

Unsure of what to order, I looked at Kuhi with hopeful eyes.

"I am ordering a black coffee," she said swiftly. "Want the same for you?"

I gave her a confused look. I wasn't fond of coffee, or anything remotely associated with coffee, but I couldn't think of a better response than a hesitant yes.

"Yes… sure, I love coffee," I said, forcing a smile.

"Sure?" she asked, an arrested look on her face. "Black coffee?"

"Of course!" I replied too loudly. "In fact, that's what I usually order here."

The waiter looked puzzled but decided not to say anything. She smiled and nodded at him.

"That will be all?" he asked her.

"I guess," she said, smiling at him. "Thank you."

"Noted," the waiter said, marching away.

"So," she said, shutting the menu. "How long have you been playing cricket?"

I was glad she asked; finally, a topic I could express lucidly. "Longer than I can remember," I said, gloating. "Ever since I was a kid."

"Okay," she replied, smiling at me.

"You too like cricket, don't you?" I asked her.

It was obvious since she had come to watch the match, after all. "Oh yes," she said. "I grew up in a household where the television either played cricket or the news."

We both laughed at this.

"That is really nice," I said. "Being a girl, of course."

She curled her eyebrows, and I realised it was a very stupid thing to say.

"Sorry," I fumbled. "I didn't mean that."

"It is absolutely fine," she said warmly.

"Don't worry about it, you meant no harm."

I sighed in relief.

She laughed again. There was something about her smile that I admired. I could watch her smile all day.

"You are acting so nervous," she said.

"It makes me wonder if I saw a different person on the field today."

My cheeks turned pink, and I looked down. Soon enough, our order arrived, and her eyes almost lit up.

"Surely you love your coffee more than I love cricket," I smiled.

"I cannot tell you how much. There are nights when I can barely sleep because I've had too much coffee. I mean, it's not the best thing to do, but I can barely resist," she said, almost licking her lips.

"So, you don't sleep at all?" I asked curiously.

"Of course, I do," she chortled.

"The effects don't last forever, duffer! It's not eternal."

I smiled at her. Kuhi was extremely spontaneous and lively, and the more time I spent with her, the more I stood in awe of her.

"You said you loved coffee," she said, suddenly stopping her stirring. "Tell me your crazy coffee story."

I almost gasped. If there were a list of people who even remotely enjoyed coffee in the university, I wouldn't even make it on there. I couldn't remember the last time I ordered coffee or made one.

"Oh well," I stuttered. "Yes, I have my fair share of stories too about waking up at 3:00 a.m. and making a cup of coffee," I said without looking at her.

I had almost cowered down the table, for I knew she could tell I was lying.

"Partners then," she said.

I was relieved and smiled at her.

"I bet I shall finish it faster than you," I said.

"That, only time will tell," she winked.

"Also, that is not how you drink your black coffee," she said, biting her lip as I was almost on the verge of dumping a sugar cube into my cup.

I looked embarrassed. "Oh yes," I said hastily, trying to cover up.

"I was just playing with it."

She bit her lip in amusement as if to conceal the laughter. "Haven't you played enough already today?"

I smiled sheepishly. Before I could understand what I had to do to make that intimidating potion look less frightening, she had gulped down her entire drink, and I was baffled.

I stared at her with my jaw wide open. "Okay, sorry for the mess," she said, her cheeks flushed. "Also, this is not how you drink your coffee either; no one should or can gulp it all down as fast as I did."

She instantly burst into laughter. I was already having the best day of my life, and being able to watch her laugh was the cherry on top.

"Can we redo it?" I asked once she had stopped.

She thought I was talking about her repeating the feat, while I was talking about watching her laugh again.

"Alright, go ahead," she said. "Drink!"

I took a sip and looked up at her. It was the bitterest thing I had ever tasted. I couldn't believe she drank it all so fast. The look on my face was a big giveaway that I had never had black coffee before. She didn't say anything but shook her head in amusement.

As I took another sip, she thrust her eyebrows upward and held her hands to her mouth to avoid bursting into laughter.

I shut my eyes, breathed in, and chugged it all. This time, I raised my eyebrows with wide eyes, and she laughed again.

She had no idea how beautiful she was. I wanted to tell her that; I wanted to write a book describing her magnificence, but it wasn't the time. I just wanted to bask in that moment and watch her laughter weave magic.

Maybe I could chug down a few more cups if that would make her laugh the way she did seconds back.

Slowly, it started getting dark, and I couldn't believe how fast time had passed. We walked towards the entrance of the university, taking a detour since we still had some time on our hands. We strolled for half a mile, discussing everything from her favourite books to the food she loved and her hobbies.

I listened intently, captivated by every word she said, like it was more important than anything I had ever heard.

"So, where are you from?" she asked me as we took a turn.

"Guwahati," I said. "And I know you are from Delhi."

"Woahhh!" she said, looking dazed. "Didn't see that coming…"

"I know, right?" I laughed. "Ritika told me that."

As I introspected, I realised that had it not been for Ritika, I would have never had the chance to be with Kuhi at that moment.

"She is a lifesaver," I said.

"I know," she said, though this time, her voice lacked the usual exuberance.

"Madhav," Kuhi suddenly said, looking at me. Her voice turned serious, and her smile disappeared.

"What happened?" I said, puzzled.

"Will you mind if I ask you something?" she said.

"Of course not," I replied swiftly. "Anything…"

"Are you two seeing each other?" she asked without making eye contact.

"What?" I said, my voice faltering. I was caught off guard; I hadn't expected her to ask that.

"Kuhi?" I said.

"I know… I know… I am sorry," she said, laughing but without her usual glow.

"I just asked because everyone in my class thinks she is your girlfriend," she said, trying to downplay it.

My heart almost sank when she said that.

"Ritika was the first person I knew when I got here," I said. "Okay, perhaps the second. The point is, she and I are very good friends."

"I know… I know," Kuhi repeated, her tone softer. "I swear I didn't intend to irritate you with this. I was just curious."

"I understand, Kuhi," I said calmly. "And she is just a very good friend; if she were my girlfriend, why would she drag you along to meet me after the match?" I forced a smile, trying to lighten the mood.

"What?" she said gently.

"No, no," I fumbled. "I didn't mean it like that."

She nodded slowly.

"Sorry for being nosy, though," she said, letting out a chuckle.

"Don't stress," I replied, relieved. "You can ask me anything."

"Alright then, last question," she said with a teasing smile. "Have you ever fallen for someone?"

I hesitated, searching for the right words. "Uh… yeah, once. But I think I fell too fast and too hard. It didn't work out."

Her expression changed slightly, and I could see a hint of concern in her eyes. "You are okay?" she asked softly.

"Yeah," I said, trying to convince both her and me. "A long time ago, I don't even remember now."

"Good," she replied.

We both laughed at her remark.

"Well, now that you know about my life, it's your turn," I said, trying to steer the conversation away from my awkwardness.

But before she could answer, she stopped and looked up at the sky. "Oh, look! A shooting star!" she exclaimed, pointing upwards.

My eyes widened, but I didn't see it. "Where? I don't see it!"

Kuhi laughed and rolled her eyes. "You missed it! You should've wished!"

"I already did," I said.

Her cheeks flushed.

I cleared my throat to ease the tension.

After some more time, she finally decided to break the silence.

"You didn't really have to do it," she said, trying to cut the apparent tension in the air.

"Do what?" I said, looking partially relieved, partially worried.

"You didn't really have to order what I had ordered, let alone drink all of it," she said.

"I could tell instantly how much you disliked it."

I didn't say anything for a moment.

"But you like coffee," I said, turning towards her, still walking along.

"Yeah…" she said softly. "Doesn't mean that you have to like it too."

"Yes I do," I blurted out, instantly regretting it.

The moment I said that, I bit my tongue and looked at the ground in embarrassment.

She tried hard to suppress her smile, but she couldn't.

"Stop smiling and say something," I said.

"Shut up," she said and prodded me in the elbow.

"Someone's clearly playing more than just cricket," she said, laughing.

I smiled but chose not to speak.

In the meantime, we had reached her hostel.

"When do we meet again?" I asked, hopeful.

"Soon," she replied.

I nodded, unable to suppress my grin.

"Well, it's a deal then!" she said, her laughter ringing in the cool evening air.

"Bye, Madhav," she said, waving at me.

"Bye, Kuhi," I said, waving back.

She smiled and walked into the dark alley before disappearing into the shadows.

I stood there with a smile on my face, reflecting on how wonderful the day had been. I felt like it was too good to be true. As I walked back, the world around me faded into the background, leaving only the sound of her laughter and the warmth of her presence. I knew, in that moment, I had fallen deeper for her.

Chapter 16

IF PICTURES COULD SPEAK

"So, how did it go?" Ritika asked as we sat in the cafeteria, her focus on fixing the leaky nib of her pen.

"Nothing much... Just that I've developed a liking for coffee lately," I replied, trying to keep a playful tone.

She dropped her pen abruptly, her eyes widening in disbelief. "Coffee? You?"

"Yeah, I know… crazy right," I chuckled.

"Love can have an altering effect on people, Ritika," I said playfully.

Ritika rolled her eyes, sarcasm dripping from her words. "*Eww.* You are done for, my friend."

"Ritika, stop exaggerating," I said, a blush creeping onto my cheeks.

"No, seriously," she insisted, leaning in. "What magic did Kuhi weave for you to start liking coffee?"

"Stop," I replied, taking a sip from her cup, savouring the bitterness.

"Hey, that is my cup!" she protested.

"It is mine now," I teased.

"Apparently, the phrase 'anything can happen over a cup of coffee' does hold true," she said, laughing.

"Not just any coffee," I corrected. "Black coffee."

I had never seen Ritika look more shocked. The only time she had come close to this expression was when I finally mustered the courage to ask Kuhi out after the match.

"The many faces of Madhav," she mumbled.

She finished her cup and stood up. "Off we go then..."

"Ah, back to your usual self," I laughed, relieved to see her spirit returning.

"Black coffee today; pineapple on pizza tomorrow," she scoffed.

"Hey, pineapple on pizza isn't..."

Before I could finish, she poked me in the ribs, dragging me toward the lecture hall.

"I wish they invented a device to measure your mood," I mused as we took our seats at the back of the hall.

Ritika preferred sitting in the front, but she occasionally joined me at the back, where the gossip flowed like the coffee we were drinking.

"Very funny," she sulked.

As spring arrived, Kuhi and I began exchanging texts throughout the day. Our class schedules rarely aligned, so I would often text her during my lectures, sneaking glances at the professor while typing away. By the end of the month, I had mastered the art of texting without looking.

"Don't whine if you get thrown out of class," Ritika warned one day.

"Don't worry," I said, puffing up my chest. "I am as sneaky as a ninja."

"Sure," she smirked, and of course, she was right.

I often found myself loitering in the corridors, getting caught and thrown out for using my phone.

But I wasn't complaining. I had no reason to hide my phone, and Kuhi made everything that happened to me seem so much sweeter. Each new day felt like an opportunity to spend more time with Kuhi.

I began waking up with thoughts of her and going to bed watching her profile. My nights felt incomplete without sending her a goodnight message. I was falling deeper for her, and there was no escape.

We started meeting frequently. Sometimes, I would join her at the library, where she would immerse herself in her books while I quietly admired her. Kuhi had an insatiable love for reading, and she carried a book wherever she went.

"Do you not get bored just sitting here?" she asked one day, her fingers flipping through the pages of her latest read.

"How are you so sure I am not doing anything?" I winked.

"What!" she exclaimed, startled.

"I am watching you read," I smiled.

She raised her eyebrows, her cheeks flushing.

"Kidding," I added quickly.

"I just enjoy the silence in here," I said.

"Right," she said, punching my arm playfully and returning her focus to the pages.

My day wouldn't go well if I didn't get punched by her at least a couple of times.

"How many books have you read till now?" I asked casually as we walked back to our hostel.

"I am not sure… maybe five hundred," she said, looking up as if trying to conjure a memory. "I try to read at least thirty each year."

"THIRTY?" I said, eyes wide. "How is that even possible?"

"Only thirty," she said, joyfully skipping and hopping on one leg, occasionally twirling as she strolled. I watched her with a smile, simply admiring the carefree energy she radiated.

"Why are you always so happy?" I asked as we reached the gate of her hostel.

"I don't know," she replied cheerfully. "I like being happy... Books make me happy... Right now, I am happy."

Yes, books made her happy, but what truly filled me with joy was seeing her happiness. Kuhi was quietly becoming a part of my daily routine, and I couldn't wait for her to become my habit.

April passed swiftly as Kuhi and I explored the city together. Beyond her love for books, she enjoyed discovering new places. We started spending more and more time together, and gradually, I found myself seeing less of Prachurjya and Ritika.

People started asking if Kuhi was my girlfriend, and I often found myself spending several minutes convincing them she wasn't. Secretly, I wished she was, but whenever someone asked her, she just laughed it off.

One day, a senior inquired if I was seeing Kuhi. Though I denied it, he sternly advised me to keep my distance from her. When I told Kuhi about it, we shared a good laugh.

"I want you to know, if I ever get strangled in my sleep, it will be because of you," I joked.

"Don't worry, no one will touch you. I am here," she said nonchalantly.

"What?" My heart skipped a beat.

"Well, I mean, I'll strangle them first," she fumbled, her face flushing.

"Right," I chuckled.

One fine day in the middle of the month, Kuhi and I decided to see a movie together. She was thrilled, having waited for this for a long time.

"There isn't a single *Shah Rukh Khan* movie I haven't watched at least three times," she declared, her eyes sparkling.

"I am sure," I replied, unsure of how to respond.

"What's your favourite SRK movie?" she asked, excitement bubbling in her voice.

"*Maine Pyaar Kiya*," I whispered.

"That's not an SRK movie!" she frowned, disappointment on her face.

"Was I talking about a movie?" I teased.

"Idiot," she said, half-embarrassed.

"Kidding," I reassured her.

"Enough of the jokes," she said. "Hurry up, let's take our seats. We wouldn't want to be late!"

"Right," I sighed, following her lead.

We arrived at the same cinema where Ritika had seen my texts months earlier. In hindsight, I was grateful for that day—if it hadn't happened, I wouldn't have been sitting there with Kuhi at that very moment.

As the movie started, Kuhi was transfixed on the screen, while I was captivated by her. With every scene, her reactions shifted—she clutched her handbag tightly, held her breath, and then exhaled deeply. Her smile lit up the dark hall whenever her favourite star appeared. I didn't need to watch the movie; her expressions narrated the whole story.

During the film, her attention remained glued to the screen, allowing me to sneak glances at her.

"That was wonderful, wasn't it?" she exclaimed as we exited the theatre.

"Surreal," I replied, still caught up in the moment.

"Spectacular," she added, her eyes gleaming.

"Beautiful," I said swiftly.

"Ummm… what?" she replied, confused.

I shook my head vigorously.

"Hey, Kuhi, I've got an idea," I said, excitement bubbling inside me. "Would you like to go to the park nearby after lunch?"

"Why not?" she responded eagerly.

We stopped at *Saffron*, a restaurant near the cinema. As usual, she ordered her ritual coffee, while I decided to skip it this time.

"Are you sure you don't want one?" she mocked. "I was under the impression you were a fan."

I quickly dashed toward the restroom, her laughter trailing behind me.

Once we finished lunch, we decided to walk to the park. But with the sun blazing overhead, we opted for a rickshaw instead.

At the park, Kuhi transformed into her playful self, running toward the swings and asking me to push her as high as I could. When she approached the see-saw, disappointment washed over her as the guard informed her it was for kids only. Despite her best attempts at negotiation, she returned to the bench beside me, clicking her tongue in frustration.

"Didn't quite go as planned?" I teased.

She frowned.

"Hey," I said, trying to lighten her mood. "How about I take a few pictures of you?"

Her eyes lit up at the suggestion. "Yes! It's been ages since I had someone take my pictures."

"Disclaimer: I am not a professional photographer, so don't expect much," I said nervously.

"Do I look like a model to you? Just tap on your phone," she quipped.

"Well, you do look like a model to me," I teased.

She smirked. "Flirt."

"Come on now, we have pictures to click," she said, pulling me by my arm. Within minutes, she found a perfect spot near a lake, where the setting sun cast a golden glow over the water.

"Come on, quick, before the light fades," she urged.

She posed, and I clicked away.

"Where's that smile when you need it?" I called out.

"You are making me nervous," she shouted back.

I laughed, and she smiled.

At that moment, she looked more beautiful than ever. She laughed, posed, and twirled as I took pictures, utterly mesmerised by her beauty.

As the sun dipped lower, casting warm colours, I captured her joy and carefree spirit in every click.

"Okay, I think I've got some great ones," I said, reviewing the pictures.

"You better," she replied, playful yet serious. "If they are bad, you'll have to take them again."

"Maybe a few bad ones will slip through then," I joked.

"Wow, these pictures are sassy."

"Of course," she grinned. "What's life without a bit of sass?"

I smiled, quietly in awe of her.

As we were leaving the park, she suddenly said, "Hey, we forgot to take a picture together."

My heart skipped a beat, but I tried to act cool.

"You are right."

"Then click, idiot," she laughed.

I inched closer to her, opening the camera. As we both came into frame, I found myself starstruck, seeing the two of us together for the first time.

"Where's that smile when you need it?" she teased, echoing my earlier words.

I raised my eyebrows, and she reciprocated.

"What are you looking at?" she asked, noticing my gaze.

"You," I winked.

She tried to resist smiling but couldn't.

"Don't Shakespeare me," she grinned. "I don't understand your silly references."

"What is the point of reading all those books then?" I laughed.

"Shut up and click," she said, punching my arm lightly.

As the day faded, casting the park in soft hues, I realised just how much I was enjoying her company. The park, with its laughter and playfulness, had turned into a canvas of golden memories.

"I can't believe how much fun today was," Kuhi said, her eyes twinkling as we took the last bus back to the university.

"Let's do it again sometime," I suggested, unable to hide my grin.

"Deal," she smiled. "Next time, we are getting ice cream, no coffee!"

"Absolutely!" I agreed, feeling a sense of happiness swell within me.

Once we reached the university, I walked Kuhi to her hostel, then made my way back to mine.

Back in my room, I looked at the picture we had taken together and smiled. Just then, a text from Kuhi popped up.

"Make sure to send me all the pictures."

"Yes, ma'am," I replied.

Then I proceeded to send her every single one, including the one of us together.

I finally gave the photo one last glance before heading out to Prachurjya's room.

Chapter 17

THE LAST EXAM TOGETHER

"Do you think I should tell her?" I asked, avoiding eye contact.

Ritika and I found ourselves alone in the deserted classroom during an off period. Instead of heading to the canteen or the library, we decided to stay put.

Ritika, engrossed in her phone, took a moment before setting aside her square-shaped glasses and giving me a stern look. Surprised by how different she appeared without them, I commented,

"You look like a completely different person without them."

"Shut up," she retorted.

"What were you saying?"

"What?" I said.

"You just mentioned saying something to someone," she said, glancing at a text on her phone from the corner of her eye.

130

"Oh, you heard that," I sneered. "I thought…"

"Get to the point," she interrupted.

"Her," I said with a shrug.

"Kuhi, you mean?" she asked bluntly.

"Well… yes," I said. "Do you think I should tell her what I feel about her?"

She sighed, put on her spectacles, and looked me dead in the eye.

"But are you sure?"

"Well… I don't know…" I stuttered. "This is why I am asking you."

"What's the date today?" she asked.

I was thrown by her question.

"The 10th of May," I said, looking baffled. "But what does that have to do with anything?"

"See," she said, "today is the 10th of May."

Unsure of what she meant, I started to feel restless.

"I am already confused. What does the 10th of May have to do with what I asked you?" I asked.

"The 10th of May, Madhav," she emphasised. "There is only a week left before the final exams."

"I really don't think this is the most appropriate time."

"Take my advice or leave it," she added with a smug face.

I didn't like her advice very much, but I knew Ritika was right.

"Also, backlogs don't make a very good lover," she laughed.

"The last person Kuhi would want to be with, in my opinion, is a romantic daft."

"Do well to not be one."

"Yeah... whatever," I said, shaking my head.

"Someone apparently isn't very good at taking advice," she quipped.

I chose not to respond.

"So, when?" I said after a pause.

"I don't know," she said. "At least not now."

Then in a particularly serious tone, she said, "Besides, how sure are you that she feels the same way about you?"

I paused, this time for longer. Ritika's question opened the floodgate of doubts. I wanted to think Kuhi felt the same, but the answer was a resounding NO. We loved each other's company, but did she see me differently? I wasn't sure about that either.

"Does she see me the same way I see her?" These words kept echoing in my mind.

"I don't know, Ritika," I said, scratching my head.

"I mean, we go out a lot, she is really nice to me, we have fun together but..."

"Exactly..." Ritika interjected. "But."

"The 'but' is what you will have to figure out," she said.

"She goes out with you, both of you share a bond, a wonderful bond, I would like to assume, but Madhav, unless you are absolutely sure, don't rush it now. Remember how you once told me 'Timing is everything in cricket'? Well, timing is everything in life too. Be sure first, and only then approach her. To score a century, you will have to reach the nineties first."

I didn't blink. I listened, gazing at her, absolutely awestruck.

"What?" she said, looking bewildered.

"Ritika… I swear to God, if you ever need an alternate career, you can start making motivational videos," I laughed.

"You would be famous and rich."

"Pay me for my advice then," she laughed.

"Anyway, I am flattered," she said. "Don't worry, it will work out. If it feels like it wouldn't, come see me for another session of *'Motivation with Ritika'*."

"Right," I said, sneering at her.

She poked me hard in my ribs and said, "Come on, I am hungry, let's get something to eat."

"Ouch!" I let out a shrill.

"Cafeteria?" I asked.

"Do you know of a better place?" she said coolly.

"Oh, Ritika," I said in a muffled voice, following her towards the cafeteria.

With only a few days until the final exam, Ritika helped me with my lessons like last time. She was extremely bright, and studying alongside her meant that I got all the important notes needed. Every day, she would send me a list of problems to solve, and what seemed daunting at first became manageable, largely thanks to her.

Unlike last time, Prachurjya decided not to leave it up to luck and joined us occasionally at the library. However, he would often fall asleep in between lessons, waking up to find us filming his light snores on my phone.

Gradually, yet very steadily, we formed a wonderful bond, and I slowly began to appreciate every little thing that was happening in my life.

In the days leading up to the exams, Kuhi and I saw less of each other; she was also busy preparing hard. We decided to postpone our outings until after the exams, but during brief meetings for lunch, she shared her study schedule with enthusiasm.

"So, is Ritika being a good teacher?" Kuhi asked enthusiastically.

"Oh yes," I exclaimed.

"She is wonderful. I wouldn't have covered half the course without her."

She beamed at me and said, "I hope you do well."

I gently nodded.

"Both of us will do well," I said, tapping her on the wrist.

Soon enough, the exams arrived. It was our German language paper, and Kuhi and I were in the same hall since it was our common subject. Once this paper was over, it would mean that Kuhi and I wouldn't share the same classroom together for a very long time.

That morning, I waited outside her hostel, and we strolled towards the hall together.

"Remember, '*eins*' is one, '*zwei*' is two, and..." she said while counting them on her fingers.

"'*Drei*' is three," I said, smiling at her.

"Not bad," she said playfully, punching my arm.

"Someone's about to ace their exam."

We reached the department and entered the hall together. I wished her luck right before we took our seats—hers in the second row of the third column towards the extreme right of the hall, mine next to Parag on the fourth bench of the middle column.

I looked at her, and just before the bell rang, she smiled at me, and we started putting pen to paper. We wrote for nearly two hours, stopping only once the final bell rang.

Once we had handed over the sheets to the invigilator, we walked out together.

"So, it went well, right?" I asked her as we walked past the corridor towards the exit.

"Yeah... kind of," she replied, her expression grim.

"You look a bit unhappy, Kuhi," I said. "What happened?"

"No..." she said, her tone disappointed. "Nothing much."

I was puzzled but didn't want to upset her further by insisting.

"Kuhi," I said softly.

She looked at me.

"I am going to miss us not being in the same class," I said calmly.

"I wish this class happened every day."

For a moment, I thought I saw her eyes well up, but she smiled.

"Yes," she said. "Doesn't mean we would see each other any less though!"

"Correct," I said with a wide smile.

We exchanged smiles as we walked out of the building.

"I can't wait for the night of the 26th," Prachurjya said, scratching his head as he lay on the bed.

I was in his room the night before the next exam, the four of us preparing.

Our exams were ending on the 26th of May, and Prachurjya was already making plans for the vacation ahead.

"Neither can I," Ashish added.

It was almost midnight, and Prachurjya had yawned at least a thousand times in the past hour.

"Right," said Biswajyoti. "Let's get through the exams, and we will all be good."

"Also, you better study. By the looks of it, you aren't going to do very well tomorrow unless you pull an 'all-nighter'."

"Shut up, Biswa," Prachurjya shot back sharply. "If I don't go to bed now, I am definitely going to miss the test tomorrow. Low marks over no marks any day."

Biswajyoti shook his head, but by then, he had already gotten used to Prachurjya's antics. Another half hour had passed when Biswajyoti finally declared that he was done studying.

"Thank goodness," Prachurjya said, instantly pulling the blanket over himself.

"What are you doing on the 27th, Madhav?" Ashish asked as we walked towards our room. He lived a floor above me.

"Going home?"

"Oh no… I am staying back," I said.

"The Inter-University Tournament is coming up."

"Oh wow," he said. "Almost forgot."

"But what about the 27th?"

He had a strange smile on his face.

"What is so intriguing about the 27th specifically?" I asked him.

Ashish was often stranger than strange, and I could never fully understand him. I would try to keep my distance, but since he was close to Biswajyoti and Prachurjya, I couldn't avoid him. However, I was seriously concerned when he mentioned '27th of May.'

"Nothing really," he said. "It is just that I thought we could all have fun together. Most of us are leaving on the 28th."

"Oh no… no," I said, clearing my throat. "I have plans."

"Of course," he said hysterically.

"Bye, Madhav."

"Bye," I said and entered my room feeling a little anxious.

"Does he know about my plan?" I thought. "How could he? Maybe I am just overthinking."

"Strange guy," I sighed.

The 27th of May was unlike any other day; it was Kuhi's birthday—a date that had taken on special significance ever since she had shared it with me. With less than a fortnight to go, I had meticulously planned every detail of how I would celebrate her day. Excitement bubbled within me as I eagerly awaited the clock to strike twelve on that day, marking the start of a celebration that I hoped would be unforgettable.

Chapter 18

27TH OF MAY

Restlessness gripped me as I paced back and forth in my corridor, the countdown to midnight ticking away. As each minute passed, my anxiety heightened.

"Breathe," I reminded myself, glancing at my watch. Forty-five minutes remained until midnight. I had rehearsed my words, learned to play the "Happy Birthday" tune on a borrowed guitar, and confirmed with Neha about hiding Kuhi's birthday cake in her room. Neha was Kuhi's roommate. Everything was in place, yet my heart pounded with anticipation.

"Thirty seconds to go," I whispered, taking a deep breath. The phone rang several times before Kuhi finally answered.

"First one to wish me," she exclaimed. "I knew it was going to be you."

"*Sshhhh*," I said, playfully interrupting her.

"Okay!" she laughed. "Not the words I quite expected, but okay."

"I want you to hold on to your breath and maybe your hat, if you are wearing one," I said. "Now just listen. No words from you."

"Ah-ha," she teased. "This is interesting."

Clearing my throat, I filled my lungs and began. "Happy Birthday to you," I sang, my fingers plucking the guitar strings like a rookie.

Kuhi gasped softly in surprise but remained quiet. I continued until the song was complete. I had spent a month learning to play the tune, and before that, I had never even touched a guitar.

"Madhav," she uttered, her voice trembling with happiness once I stopped.

"Yes, Kuhi," I replied, feeling the warmth in her voice through the phone.

"I can't tell you what this means to me," she whispered, her voice thick with emotion. "No one has ever done something like this for me."

"Well, they have been foolish not to," I responded with a smile, wishing I could see the joy on her face.

"Oh, by the way, this isn't everything," I added mischievously.

"What?" she asked excitedly.

"Do me a favour," I said. "Look at Neha and say 'Hi, Neha…'"

Confused but curious, she followed my instructions. Moments later, I heard Neha wishing her and unveiling the cake I had arranged. Alongside the cake was a card that read, *"There will never be another Kuhi,"* written in bright colours.

"Oh my God, Madhav, you didn't have to do this," she said, her voice breaking with emotion.

"Thank you, Madhav. This truly means so much to me."

"Don't say that…" I said calmly. "It's your birthday, and you have no idea how long I have been waiting for the 27th of May."

After a brief pause, I added, "You know, a lot of people are perhaps waiting to wish you. I would love to chat all night, but I'll let you enjoy your moment. Happy Birthday, Kuhi."

"No, stay until I cut the cake," she insisted.

"Sure," I said, unable to suppress my grin.

I stayed on the call for another fifteen minutes, listening to the chorus of birthday wishes from her hostel mates. As the room quieted, Kuhi's voice softened. "Madhav, honestly… thank you so much. You've made my birthday unforgettable."

"Well…" I teased, "Just make sure you are ready by eleven tomorrow morning."

"Are we going somewhere?" she asked, her voice bubbling with excitement.

"You will find out tomorrow," I said, leaving her in suspense.

Before she could probe further, I disconnected the call with a wide smile. I had managed to make her birthday special, and it felt like a sweet victory.

The next morning, I woke to the echoing sound of my alarm. I checked my phone: 27th May. As I replayed the events of the previous night, a smile crept across my face. This was the day I had been planning for weeks.

At ten minutes to eleven, I stepped outside my room to find Kuhi already waiting by her hostel gate. Dressed in a snowy white dress that shimmered in the sunlight, her hair fell in soft waves around her shoulders. She looked effortlessly beautiful, and for a moment, I was left speechless.

"Wow, you look stunning today," I said, my gaze fixed on her.

"Today?" she asked with a playful smile. "Do I not look pretty otherwise?"

"Well…" I winked at her.

She responded with a playful elbow to my ribs.

"Ouch, that hurt," I giggled.

"Happy Birthday, Miss Kuhi Sharma," I said, bowing theatrically.

"Thank you," she grinned. "But you've said it more than a dozen times since last night."

"Yeah, and all I've gotten in return is bruised ribs," I sulked, feigning pain. "Life is unfair."

She laughed. "So, where are we going?"

"You will see soon enough," I said with a sly smile.

"Quite the planner, I see," she said.

"Also, this must be the first time someone is taking me out on my own birthday. Usually, it's the other way around," she remarked.

"I am telling you, Kuhi, you really hang out with the wrong set of people," I said casually.

"Shut up," she sneered.

I took her to *The Crimson*, a fine dining place in town.

Kuhi had once mentioned it during one of our long walks,

"Someday, I would like to take all my friends to The Crimson. It's so elegant."

As we stepped into the restaurant, soft jazz played in the background, and the warm lighting cast a golden hue over everything. Kuhi's eyes widened as she took in the ambiance.

"This place is gorgeous," she whispered.

"I know," I said, pleased with her reaction.

The waiter arrived with our coffee—black, just the way she liked it.

"Still drinking this?" Kuhi teased, remembering what had happened the last time.

"What can I say? It has grown on me," I replied, taking a sip.

We spent the next few hours talking and laughing as she shared stories from her past birthdays, including a hilarious incident where she mistook vinegar for water and a prank that went wrong.

As we finished our meal, the waiter returned with a large basket, carefully placing it in front of Kuhi.

"What's this?" she asked, eyes wide.

"Just the final piece of the birthday puzzle," I said nonchalantly. "Open it."

With curiosity, she began unwrapping the basket, revealing a dozen books—all titles she had been eager to read, a list I had carefully gathered from our conversations.

"Oh my God, this is amazing!" she exclaimed, her face lighting up. "But I can't accept this."

"Sorry, non-returnable, non-refundable," I teased.

As she continued rifling through the books, she froze. Buried beneath the pile was a white instant camera.

"Madhav, you didn't..." Her voice trailed off, overwhelmed.

"I hope this helps us make memories everywhere we go," I said gently.

"No, I can't take this," she said.

"Okay then," I replied, taking the camera from her hands.

Before she could react, I snapped a picture of her without warning. The camera clicked, capturing not just a photo but a moment—one that would be etched in my memory forever.

"Like I said, *non-refundable, non-negotiable,*" I teased.

"This is the most beautiful birthday of my life," she whispered, clutching my wrist. "Thank you."

As she held my wrist, in that moment, I felt like I had conquered the world. A profound connection enveloped us. It was a moment beyond words, a snapshot that even the instant camera couldn't have fully encapsulated.

Life has a way of surprising us when we least expect it. I set out to give Kuhi the best birthday moment, yet she, unknowingly, gave me the best moment of my life. In that enchanting moment, I realized that there could never truly be another Kuhi.

Chapter 19

RITIKA'S BIG SECRET

"Use your bottom hand more; that way you are going to have a bit more power behind your shots," Anuj advised as we practised in the nets.

I nodded gently and re-adjusted my gloves.

Anuj and I had spent the past few days buried in cricket practice, gearing up for the upcoming Inter-University tournament. With the university nearly deserted due to the vacation, it was just the two of us left on campus, along with Ritika and the rest of my teammates, who stayed back for an internship. When we weren't on the field, we were locked in intense gaming sessions in his room.

With Kuhi having flown home and Prachurjya and Biswajyoti also away, my companions were limited to Anuj and Ritika. Ritika on the other hand, had to stay back for a few weeks due to an internship that she picked up. However, owing to schedule conflicts, we barely saw one another.

Kuhi and I hadn't spoken much since she left for home. During the day, when she was free, I would be on the field, and by the time I was done, she would already be asleep.

One evening, after a practice session ended earlier than usual, I decided to call her. Her voice sounded different—what usually lit up an entire room suddenly seemed dull and worried. There was something off about the way she spoke.

"Hi, Madhav," she greeted weakly. Her usual vibrancy had been replaced by an underlying fragility.

"Kuhi, are you okay?" I asked with genuine concern.

"Yeah, just a bad headache," she admitted, her voice quavering.

"Are you taking any medicine?" I asked, worried.

"Not really, but I am feeling better now," she replied, though the tone of her voice suggested otherwise.

"Your voice says something different," I remarked, still uneasy.

Trying to lighten the mood, she said, "How about you fly down here to check for yourself, Mister?" She attempted to laugh but was interrupted by a violent cough.

"I wish I could, but you know how long I have been waiting for this tournament," I explained.

"You sound really sick, Kuhi."

"Not really, but I'll still get my tests done. Also, I was just joking. You will do well in the tournament," she said, quickly changing the subject.

"Thanks," I replied, though my tone remained heavy with concern. "Take care of yourself, promise?"

"Promise," she affirmed.

"Now go rest, or else I will really come to Delhi," I teased.

"Sure," she said, before hanging up.

There was something unsettling about our conversation. Her voice, so oddly different, lingered in my thoughts long after the call ended.

I sat down, absentmindedly twirling my phone, replaying the conversation in my head. Just then, my phone buzzed—it was Ritika.

"Yo, what's up?" she asked casually.

"Hi... nothing much," I replied. "Just had a call with Kuhi. She is not feeling well. Done for the day?"

"Don't ask, I am exhausted," she sighed. "What's wrong with Kuhi?"

"I am not sure," I began, but she interrupted.

"Do one thing—get ready in a couple of minutes, and we can talk about it in person."

"I am a bit tired," I said. "Maybe tomorrow?"

"In a minute and a half," she commanded, abruptly ending the call.

I shook my head, already used to Ritika's ways. Without protest, I got up and dressed.

As I strolled out of my room, another text buzzed my phone: ***COME OUT NOW.***

Feeling the urgency, I rushed downstairs and out of the hostel.

"Remind me, what was your name again?" she teased as I reached the meeting spot, clearly out of breath.

"No time for your jokes, just get to the point," I said, still panting.

"No, I mean, not every girl has Madhav as a name," she quipped playfully.

"What?" I asked, confused.

"Well, with the time you take to get ready, you could put all models to shame," she teased.

"Ritika," I sighed.

"Yeah?" she replied, avoiding eye contact.

"That was the worst joke you have ever made," I laughed.

"I can't help it if you don't have a sense of humour," she retorted, a playful smirk dancing on her lips.

"Never mind, come on, I don't have all day."

We strolled toward a small lake nestled within the campus and settled on an empty bench beside it. The lake, known as *'Niribili'* glimmered softly in the fading light, its gentle ripples creating a serene ambiance. With the sun having dipped below the horizon, the twilight cast a tranquil glow over the water, making it feel like a hidden gem—often holding secrets of whispered conversations and shared laughter, just in front of the Vice Chancellor's bungalow.

After a moment of silence, Ritika finally spoke.

"So, tell me what happened," she said, breaking a wafer in half and handing me a piece.

"Nothing too serious," I began, munching on the wafer. "The tournament is coming up, and I am a bit anxious."

"And?" she prompted.

"And what?" I asked.

Suddenly, a rustling noise interrupted our conversation. I turned around, sensing an eerie presence behind the bushes.

"What?" Ritika asked.

"I thought I heard something," I said, slightly on edge.

"Just a cat or a dog, maybe," Ritika dismissed it. "Now, will you tell me or not?" she asked, offering me another piece of the wafer.

"Stop messing around," she said.

I decided to ignore the sound and focus back on her.

"The thing is, I called Kuhi a while ago," I explained. "She sounded weak, almost off."

"Is she unwell?" Ritika asked, sounding concerned.

"I don't know," I shrugged. "She said it's just a headache, but I am not sure."

"Didn't she tell you what's wrong?"

"Not really," I replied.

Ritika's expression shifted to one of seriousness. "She will be fine," she reassured me, her hand briefly brushing against mine in a comforting gesture.

"I hope so," I said, my uncertainty still evident.

"Maybe she is just missing you," Ritika teased, trying to lighten the mood.

"Maybe," I nodded, though the worry lingered.

Just as I was about to mention how abruptly she had disconnected the call; Ritika suddenly shifted the conversation.

"Now wait, let me show you something."

Ritika eagerly showed me pictures of her workplace. She had clicked tons of photos from her internship, excited about her first professional experience.

As I scrolled through the images, she narrated every detail about her office. After what felt like endless swiping, I became familiar with every nook and cranny of her desk.

However, in a moment of embarrassment, she snatched her phone as I stumbled upon a picture—a selfie with a boy holding her by her shoulder.

"Wait a minute," I said.

My eyes lit up.

"Ritika," I said, looking at her. She avoided eye contact, her ears turning pink.

"Who is that guy?"

"What am I missing out on?"

I quickly muscled my way and snatched her phone back from her hands.

My heart nearly skipped a beat when I recognized the boy in the photo.

"That's Rohan, isn't it?" I asked, still zooming in on the picture.

"No," she denied, her voice faint.

"I know it's him," I insisted.

After a moment of silence, she sighed in defeat. "Fine, yes, it's Rohan."

I had never seen Ritika look so embarrassed.

This revelation marked a rare moment where I could finally have an upper hand on Ritika.

I couldn't help but feel excited but also curious.

"So, tell me all about it," I said.

At first, she hesitated, but with a bit of coaxing, she opened up.

"It has only been about a week," she confessed. "We went out right after the semester ended."

"And you didn't tell me?" I asked, slightly disappointed.

"Did you tell me about Kuhi right away?" she shot back but immediately softened, embarrassed by her admission.

"Okay, fine," she sighed. "I wanted to tell you, but I didn't know how."

"I am your best friend, Ritika," I frowned, pretending to be upset. "Or am I?"

"Don't be silly," she said, resting her head on my shoulder and breaking another wafer in two, handing me one. "You are my best friend; I just didn't know how to bring it up."

"It's fine," I said, patting her on the back. "But this is big news!" I grinned mischievously. "Prachurjya will go nuts when he finds out."

"No!" she said, horrified. "You can't tell him now."

I raised an eyebrow. "Why not?"

"Because he is the last person who can keep a secret," she explained.

After thinking it over, I realised she had a point.

"Okay, fine," I relented.

"Thank you," she said, almost hugging me in excitement.

"Easy there," I smirked. "I am not Rohan."

"Shut up," she playfully smacked my arm.

"Let's get something to eat," she suggested, visibly relieved.

"Only if you give me all the details while we wait," I teased.

"Deal," she said, pulling my cheeks.

"Wow, the excitement," I laughed.

"Very funny," she replied.

We then share a moment of laughter, getting up from the bench and walking out of the dark alley, finally stepping into the brighter lights, leaving behind the worries of the day.

Chapter 20

THE END OF DREAMS

The next morning, sunlight poured through my window, casting a warm glow across the room. It was a bright, promising day, yet my heart felt heavy with anticipation. With a sense of urgency, I hurried through my morning routine, devouring breakfast before dashing off to the ground for warm-up drills.

"Ready?" Anuj's voice cut through the crisp morning air as we jogged along the boundary ropes.

"Absolutely," I replied with a nod.

As we completed a few rounds around the ropes, the sun beat down relentlessly, its harsh rays scorching the back of our necks.

Anuj, clad in his whites and donning a round hat to shield himself from the intense heat, glanced towards the sky.

"Looks like we are in for a tough one today," he remarked before turning his attention back to our circuit.

The final squad was to be announced that evening, and despite feeling confident about securing a spot, I couldn't shake the '*what if*' that lingered in my mind.

The previous night had been fraught with worry. Kuhi's test results had come in: she was diagnosed with dengue and required immediate attention. She was transferred to a local medical facility for better care. Communication was sparse, limited to sporadic updates from a common friend who lived nearby. Bedridden and weak, Kuhi's condition weighed heavily on my mind, a constant source of concern amidst the looming competition.

On the other hand, Ritika had only a couple of days left before her internship ended. She would then be flying back home too.

As practice commenced that day, the routine of fielding drills followed by batting in the nets unfolded. I picked up the new ball and marked my run-up, but I heard the coach call out from behind.

"Madhav, pad up," he said. "I want to watch you bat today."

I paused, unsure how to respond. I had barely slept the previous night, and my confidence was wavering. Still, I couldn't risk disappointing the coach with the squad announcements so close. I marched toward the boundary ropes to gear up.

As I walked in to bat, Anuj's sharp voice caught my attention.

"Madhav!" he called. "You are forgetting something."

Confused, I looked at him. He shook his head and handed me my helmet.

"Sorry, just a little preoccupied," I replied.

"No problem," he said with a smile.

"A cracked skull won't help your cause in Odisha. Never forget the helmet," he joked.

I nodded and put the helmet on. The sun hung overhead; its intensity was almost blinding.

The session began, each delivery met with varying degrees of success. However, I missed more deliveries than I connected with, occasionally watching my stumps cartwheel. Frustration simmered beneath the surface as I struggled to find my rhythm, the weight of exhaustion bearing down on me.

In the adjacent nets, the other batsmen were in top form. Jayanta was effortlessly thrashing bowlers, a stark reminder of my own shortcomings.

"Anything wrong?" Anuj asked midway through the session.

I shook my head, unable to articulate my exasperation.

With each missed opportunity, I could see disappointment mounting on the coach's face. My ticket to Odisha felt blurrier with every miss.

As the session ended, I retreated to the pavilion, my disappointment palpable. I was swept up in a range of emotions: fear, anxiety, tiredness.

"I can still bowl," I muttered half-heartedly to myself in a desperate attempt at comfort.

"But so can the other bowlers," a voice replied inside me.

Not knowing what to do, I joined the fielders circling the net.

Anuj approached me again.

"What's the problem, buddy?" he inquired, his voice laced with concern.

"I don't know," I admitted, vulnerability creeping in.

"I just feel a little dizzy."

"Then you shouldn't be here," he insisted, his voice firm. "Get some rest. Don't tell the coach about the dizziness— just say you have an upset stomach."

"Why not?" I asked, curiosity piqued.

"Because that might make him think you are not fit enough to board the bus to Odisha," he explained. "At this point, the last thing you want is to plant any seeds of doubt in the coach's mind. We all have an upset stomach occasionally; he will understand."

With a wink, he ran back to his position. "Also, move back; you are too close to the batsman," he shouted over his shoulder.

I stood there for a moment, weighing my options, but decided to stay put.

"Just an off day for me," I said. "A few drinks of water, and I'll be good as new."

"But is Kuhi okay?"

"Maybe I should check on her once," I pondered aloud. "We haven't talked since last night. Maybe I should send her a song to cheer her up. Should I go take care of her? This tournament can wait—maybe next year."

Lost in a sea of uncertainty, I barely registered the thunderous crack of Kushal's shot as it tore through the netting, hurtling toward me with alarming speed.

I couldn't react in time, and before I knew it, I felt a force unlike anything I had experienced before.

In the chaos that followed, time seemed to stand still. Pain exploded behind my eyes as the ball collided with the back of my head, engulfing my senses in a blinding white-hot flash.

The world spun; I could not register anything at all. Voices echoed distantly; my vision blurred. I couldn't decipher their words. Blinking against the harsh light felt impossibly difficult as I lay flat on the ground.

"Am I dying?" I thought. "No, this cannot happen." I tried to speak, but my senses slipped from my control. I realised I had no control over anything at all.

And then, darkness descended.

As I began to wake up, my awareness slowly returned—a faint sense of consciousness trying to break through the darkness. I could hear a familiar voice, but I couldn't make sense of anything.

Blinking against the bright fluorescent lights, I saw my mother, her eyes filled with tears.

"Rubu," she exclaimed, reaching for my hand.

"How do you feel?"

I felt confused, struggling to understand what was happening. In the background, I noticed Ritika staring at me, worry etched on her face.

It hit me: I was in the hospital, but I still didn't know why.

Nothing made sense; moments back, I was on the ground, and then I found myself on the hospital bed.

"What happened, maa?" I whispered; my voice barely audible.

My mother's eyes filled with unshed tears, her voice shaky.

"God has been kind to keep you safe," she said, her words heavy with fear.

"Wow… you are making it sound like I died," I replied, trying to smile, but even that hurt in places I hadn't felt before.

"Two weeks of being unconscious and you still manage to sound silly," Ritika chimed in. "Aunty, this is why I call him an idiot."

"Excuse me… I am not an idi—" I started, but then I realised how serious this was.

"What do you mean *Two weeks of being unconscious?*" I asked, my voice filled with panic.

Suddenly, it didn't feel funny anymore.

"I have been here for two weeks?"

As bits of memory returned, I recalled that day's practice—the sickening sound of the ball hitting my head, a harsh reminder of how fragile life can be.

"You've been unconscious for two weeks, completely unresponsive," Ritika explained, her voice a mix of worry and frustration.

"Aunty, please call the doctor. In the meantime, I can give this daredevil a lesson he won't forget."

My mother nodded and left the room.

The weight of her words hit me like a wave, overwhelming me with disbelief.

Days had slipped away without me noticing.

"How is Kuhi?" I asked.

"What about my tournament? I didn't think I was hurt enough to be out for weeks. Tell me!"

"Calm down, daredevil," she said calmly.

"You will soon find out everything; just relax."

"No, wait," I insisted. "I need to see Kuhi. She needs me."

Suddenly, the smile faded from Ritika's face.

"Do you even understand how serious this is?" she shouted.

"When Prachurjya first called me, I thought he was joking. But when I got here, I was shocked. You were barely breathing, and there was blood everywhere. The doctors were worried about permanent brain damage."

"You should have been more careful, Madhav."

Her eyes filled with tears as she spoke, a mix of anger and sadness in her voice.

"You should have been more careful, Madhav," she repeated, sitting down next to my bed.

"And yes, Kuhi is okay."

I lay there, trying to process everything she had said. I couldn't wrap my head around what had happened. My dreams felt like they had gone up in flames.

"But weren't you supposed to fly back home?" I asked after a moment.

"Really?" she shot back, surprised. "That is all you have to say?"

"Thanks, Ritika," I replied, struggling to hold back my tears. "Thank you for everything."

"Idiot," she said, shaking her head with a small smile.

"Never forget the helmet... Anuj was right," I whispered softly.

It felt like I had just been on the field hours ago, but soon I realised I had lost control of my fate for weeks.

"A cracked skull won't help your cause in Odisha," those exact words of Anuj, when he had asked me to get some rest, circled my mind before I drifted off, hoping to wake up from the nightmare.

Chapter 21

TOPSY-TURVY

Sometimes, life takes an unexpected turn for the worse. It doesn't care about your plans or aspirations; it will take its own course, just as it's meant to. I was no exception; life took a sudden nosedive, catching me off guard and plunging me into a whirlwind of adversity. Everything that once seemed fine had suddenly turned to wreckage, and I barely had a chance to react. It felt as if I had fallen into my worst nightmare, with no way out. My dream of representing my university had been shattered, and all I could do was wait for another chance—the following year.

As I lay in my hospital bed, contemplating the wreckage of my aspirations, the doctor's visit deepened my despair. I had grown tired of being in the same place. It had been almost a week since I had come back to my senses, yet there was hardly any progress.

"If only I had listened to Anuj," I repeated for the hundredth time. Even Ritika had grown bored of hearing it.

"So, how do you feel now?" the doctor asked kindly. He was in his mid-thirties and wore a radiating smile.

"Better, I guess," I replied gloomily.

He nodded gently but chose not to say anything further.

"Doctor, you mentioned something the other day," I said, looking at him. "About some important tests…"

A palpable sense of unease settled over the room, thickening the air with tension. For the first time since I had met him, I saw him look at me without his usual smile.

"Okay," he breathed. "So, your mother told me all about your love for cricket."

I nodded fervently.

"I realised that what happened to you was entirely due to misfortune—something none of us can control; accidents happen," he said.

"I won't lie; it could have been a lot more serious than it looks now, but—"

He paused, and my insides lurched. I sensed something unpleasant coming my way.

"Madhav," he began, his tone solemn, "I am afraid the prognosis isn't as hopeful as we had hoped. Your injury, while not immediately life-threatening, will require extensive rehabilitation and caution in the coming years."

"I don't understand," I said, confusion evident on my face.

"Look, I know this will be difficult to hear, but you won't be able to participate in any physical activities that involve running or lifting weights for quite some time."

The moment I heard this; my eyes widened in shock.

"Listen," he continued, "You will need to be careful not to push yourself too hard; this was a traumatic injury. You are lucky to have recovered the way you have. However, if you are not cautious, things could change for the worse."

"I have informed your mother about everything she needs to know, and she has assured me that she will take care of you," he added. "But since you live away from home, it is equally important you look after yourself too."

"I'll make sure he does," Ritika chimed in from her seat.

"Great," the doctor smiled.

"You just need to rest and take it easy. Think of this as a bouncer—duck for now, and when the time comes, you will hit it out of the park."

"When you say, *'quite some time'* how long do you mean?" I asked, my voice trembling.

"As soon as you complete your recovery," he replied, offering a reassuring smile.

I couldn't muster the courage to ask anything; I just felt numb. He then stood up, patted me on the shoulder, and left.

I lay there, trying to digest the fact that I might never fulfil my dream of playing for my university or pursuing any form of sports again. The Inter-University tournament, once a beacon of hope, now loomed on the horizon like a distant memory.

Tears trickled down my cheeks, and I felt utterly devastated.

"Why me, Ritika?" I sulked, my voice barely audible above the cacophony of my thoughts.

She was teary-eyed too, knowing my love for the game. She stood at the corner, searching for the right words. Ritika, who always had an answer, seemed at a loss, grappling with the weight of my despair.

"Madhav," she finally said, settling into the chair next to my bed, "sometimes all it takes is a little courage to find your ray of hope. Life throws us curveballs that we never see coming. But you, my friend, are stronger than you know. You are a champion, and no setback can dim your spirit or resolve."

"You are going to do great; just give yourself some time. Nothing will change if you don't."

"But I didn't deserve this," I said, grieving.

"I know," she replied. "But it's alright. We can only brush off the dust and keep moving ahead when we fall. We will move on from this, and before we know it, you will be back doing what you do best."

I nodded and rubbed my eyes.

"But… it was my dream."

"Don't worry, Madhav," she said calmly. "This may seem like the end, but believe me, it is not. We will get there soon—maybe not now, but soon."

Her words, though heavy with sadness, offered a glimmer of hope, reminding me that even in the bleakest circumstances, there remained a flicker of light.

"Thanks, Ritika," I said.

"Now, stop whimpering like a child, or I might have to buy you a box of diapers instead," she joked, a playful grin spreading across her face.

We both smiled at that remark.

"See? So much better!" she said. "Don't worry! You have me. You have all of us. Things will get better before you even know it."

In the days that followed, as I was discharged, Ritika flew back to Kolkata to spend the remaining holiday time at home. Meanwhile, Prachurjya came to visit me. As I acclimated to life beyond the hospital, Ritika and Prachurjya remained constant pillars of support.

I realised how funny it was that we all have so many plans and dreams about things we can't control, yet life often has its own plans—vastly different from our expectations.

I was slowly recovering, but amid the chaos, one question weighed heavily on my mind: What about Kuhi? Despite Ritika's advice to withhold the truth, I grappled with the burden of unspoken words. Kuhi, diagnosed with dengue, was slowly recovering too, and Ritika thought it would be too much for her to handle while still being treated.

We had barely spoken during the semester break—first, her being bedridden with illness, then my injury. On most days, her phone was switched off, understandable given her weakness. Still, I hoped she would ask how I was doing, at least once. Once, I even considered defying Ritika and telling her everything that had happened, but I realised Kuhi had enough issues to deal with in her life already.

As the university prepared to reopen, a text from Kuhi reignited a flicker of hope within me: "I have to tell you a lot of things."

With anticipation, I awaited the chance to confide in her, to share the burden of my struggles and fears, and to seek solace in the warmth of her unwavering support.

I called her phone one final time a day before the university reopened, but her phone was still switched off.

"All it takes is a little courage to find your ray of hope," I reminded myself of what Ritika had said.

"Tomorrow then," I said to myself as I placed my cricket kit in the storeroom of my house, remembering the doctor's words. I would not be needing my kit bag for a long time.

Chapter 22

THE ESCALATION

Kuhi's jaw dropped, and her eyes widened as she caught sight of me for the first time in over a month and a half. A tense silence stretched between us, thick with unspoken questions.

We were sitting in the cafeteria after a long break. As usual, it was swarmed with students trying to grab a coffee or a sandwich between classes.

"What's wrong?" I asked, avoiding her gaze.

She remained silent, her expression one of disbelief as she grappled with the noticeable scar on my head.

"How could you not tell me?" she finally burst out, her eyes filled with a mix of hurt, frustration, and concern.

"Not tell you what?" I said, desperately trying to avoid addressing the obvious.

"THIS," she almost roared.

"Kuhi, calm down," I urged, trying to ease the tension. "This is nothing serious at all."

Despite her illness, she looked beautiful, though she was visibly thinner and paler. I was relieved to see her again.

"Madhav?" she exclaimed.

"Let it be, Kuhi," I said. "We have all the time in the world to talk about this; I do not wish to revisit it now."

"You should have told me. How could you keep this from me?" she demanded, her voice trembling with emotion.

"How could I have?" I shot back. For some reason, I had lost my composure. Perhaps I was frustrated too, having stayed away from her with barely any contact.

"I tried calling you countless times and sent numerous texts, but you barely cared enough to reply."

"Madhav," she said, her eyes watery. "I was sick."

"Of course you were sick," I said. "But I was in the hospital too, unconscious for two weeks. Almost dead. But the first question I asked—"

"How is Kuhi?"

"All I asked for was some form of communication, but it wasn't to be."

She stood there, looking at me as if she had a lot to say but was holding back.

"It was a nightmare," she finally spoke.

"I am sorry," I said.

I knew she had been unwell, but her tone hinted at deeper troubles.

"What happened?" I asked gently, hoping to offer some solace.

She hesitated before responding, "Nothing much. Just a rough time at the hospital for me too."

"Why didn't you reach out to me properly once you felt better?" I said softly, my tone different from moments before.

She fell silent again, avoiding my gaze.

"I assumed you were away for the tournament," she began, her voice trailing off.

"I thought we could catch up once you returned, but..."

"But what?" I prompted, sensing there was more to her hesitation.

"Nothing, forget it," she dismissed. "Anyway, tell me what happened," she said, changing the subject. "And how did the tournament go?"

"I couldn't make it of course," I admitted.

Her reaction was one of disbelief.

"What?" she said, her eyes wide.

As I recounted the events to her, she listened patiently, though she almost snapped once at me for my recklessness when I told her how Anuj had asked me to go back, but I did not listen.

I told her everything: how I couldn't sleep the night before and how I was hit by the ball. I explained my time at the hospital, how Prachurjya had come to visit, and how my mother had taken care of me.

By the time I finished, she was on the verge of tears again.

"It will all work out fine," I smiled. "Don't worry."

She smiled back and gently rubbed the back of my hand.

"As they say, *sometimes all it takes is a little courage to find your ray of hope*," I said, trying to cheer her up.

However, her smile vanished instantaneously as I said that.

She withdrew her hand abruptly.

"What?" I asked, puzzled.

"Those words..." she hesitated.

"What about them?" I prodded.

"What did you say exactly?" she retorted.

"That everything will work out fine?" I asked, confused.

"No... after that," she said, her expression stern.

"*That sometimes all it takes is a little courage to find your ray of hope*," I repeated.

"They don't sound like you, Madhav," she said, her tone uneasy.

"These are not your words."

Confusion clouded my thoughts as tension filled the air. Our earlier excitement about meeting seemed to have vanished.

"I have no idea what you mean," I said.

"Where did Ritika stay during all that time?" she asked abruptly, her tone sharp.

"Sorry?" I replied, bewildered.

"Where was she all this while?"

"I have no idea what is going on here," I said, a hint of annoyance creeping into my voice.

Frustrated by her questions, I felt she was being unreasonable, given all I had gone through.

"Where was Ritika?" she pressed.

"Are you sure she doesn't have anything for you?"

"I've told you before, and I'll say it again," I asserted firmly. "Ritika is my best friend, nothing more."

"She is my best friend, and she has always been with me, but that is just about it. Nothing more, nothing less..."

"I thought after what I went through, I would find comfort in you. I thought I could confide in you but look where we are."

"Where was Ritika, really?" she repeated.

I looked at her, and for the first time since I had known her, I felt a surge of annoyance.

She just kept staring at me, and I began to breathe heavily.

Then I snapped. I didn't know why, but the frustration brewing inside me needed to be released.

"She stood by my side when I had almost crumbled to pieces. She was the one who helped me see the brighter side when I felt I had lost everything," I continued.

"Do you even realise what it is like to have something in your hands, and before you can grasp it and hold it close, lose it the next moment?"

"I do not expect you to understand what I went through, but the least you can do is be a bit empathetic. I've had enough already; the last thing I want to do now is validate and justify my bond with Ritika."

"You said you had a terrible experience. Do you have any idea what I went through? If not for the support of the right people, I would have crumbled. But you only had dengue; you wouldn't know."

"You did not go through a nightmare; I did. You were not even bothered to reply to my texts after all."

"The doctor said I was lucky; it could have been so much more serious, perhaps lethal."

"But why would you care? All you really care about is what she feels about me. It doesn't matter if I am alive or dead."

"You know, ever since I got to know that you had dengue, I couldn't stop worrying about you. I was so occupied that at one point, I thought of giving up on the tournament to check on you. And when the ball hit me, I was still thinking about you. Who knows, if I hadn't thought of you at that moment, I would have been okay, still playing the game."

She gasped.

As soon as I said that I knew I had gone too far.

I was hit with instant regret.

"I am sorry," I said shakily. "I did not—"

"Madhav, stop," she yelled.

Tears trickled down her cheeks, and her nose had gone pink. She brushed her tears away with the sides of her palms.

People in the cafeteria turned their heads towards us curiously.

"You do not know my situation, what I have been through… what I am going through. You have said enough. I have always genuinely respected your feelings and emotions, but that does not give you the liberty to say anything you want to. Do you know what I have been through? Do you even know what it is like to be in my shoes right now? You have no idea."

"And yes, you may have lost your tournament or maybe a year, but I endured a great deal too. You know, Madhav, the problem is we humans are often too quick to write off others' pains and sufferings. It is only when we go through the same that we realise that *'terrible experiences'* are sometimes subjective as well."

"Thank you, Madhav; it was a pleasure," she said, and walked away.

As she walked away, a profound sense of loss washed over me. Part of me wanted to stop her, but I could not—or maybe I did not.

Things around me seemed to have gone silent the farther she walked from me. The slow murmurs filled the hall once again, and I made my way out as well, with Ritika and Prachurjya following close behind.

Chapter 23

BREAKING THE NEWS

"How could you even do that?" Ritika slammed the table so hard that the jug almost tumbled down.

We were sitting at *'Café Edona'* that evening, a few hundred metres from the university gate. Ritika had dragged me along because I had locked myself up and refused to talk about anything that had happened that afternoon.

"Can we not talk about this, please?" I said.

"Please, Madhav, be reasonable," she said, cracking her knuckles. "What you did was not right. You must apologise."

"Ritika," I growled. "I have always valued your opinion, but I really would not want you to get into this, please."

She took a deep breath, adjusted her voice, and said, "Madhav, she was seriously ill, and besides—"

"Besides what?" I clenched my jaw.

"I don't ask for much, but the least I can expect from Kuhi is a bit of empathy. I mean, I deserve that from her." "And speaking of which, did you not hear what the doctor said?"

"That a little here and there could have been fatal for me."

"Ritika, do you realise what it feels like to not be able to go to the field? Do you know how terribly difficult it is for me to watch my teammates run around the pitch, something that I should have been doing too? Do you realise what it is like to not be able to run, jog, or even walk long distances?"

It was getting difficult to speak as my voice started to choke with my own tears.

"Madhav, please calm down and listen to me," she said empathetically.

"I was there with you. I saw what had happened, and I know how terrible it was, but repeating the same thing will not change what happened. It has been difficult for each one of us, but for God's sake, stop pitying yourself."

"What do you mean?" I said broodingly.

"Well…" she continued.

"You do not know what Kuhi has gone through either."

"She has gone through a lot, so for one last time, stop comparing your situation with hers. You are a strong person, and I promise you, if there is ever a situation where you think you are all alone, you will find me by your side."

I nodded gently.

"Now, chin up and smile."

I looked at her with hopeful eyes and smiled awkwardly.

She shook her head and said,

"I would not call it a smile, but well, it's better than watching you cry."

"Believe me, you look very ugly while crying."

I rolled my eyes in disdain.

"Now, about Kuhi…" she said, but before she could complete, Rohan sneaked up from behind and covered Ritika's eyes with his hands.

"There she is," he said dramatically and grinned at her.

Rohan was the same guy from the bus who had offered his seat to Ritika, and they were seeing each other—a fact Ritika had tried very hard to conceal but ultimately failed.

"How are you?" he said, looking at me and smiling widely again.

"Fine," I said flatly.

"Come on, have a seat," said Ritika.

Instantly, he pulled a chair from the table next to us and joined us in a flash.

It was a warm day, and I was surprised to see him wear a flashy jacket with ripped jeans.

"Came from a ride?" I said.

"Nope," he said.

"This is my style," he winked and looked at Ritika.

"Right?" he said to her.

"Right," she said, looking a little embarrassed.

"Right, so I am sure you guys know each other, but yes, Rohan—he is Madhav, Madhav—he is Rohan."

He shook my hand and turned his head towards Ritika, smiling.

"Of course, I know all about you," he said.

"Ritika has told me everything about you."

As he spoke, his head swayed from side to side, and his expressions changed with each word he spoke, something which I found extremely annoying.

"So, Madhav, I hope you are alright, my friend."

"Terribly sorry for what happened; it is a shame you had to miss the tournament."

I almost flinched but managed to smile.

"Yeah, next time maybe," I said hopefully.

"But didn't the doctor say otherwise…" he said until Ritika interrupted him.

"ROHAN," she growled.

"Yes… yes," he fumbled.

"Next time surely."

"So, how is Kuhi holding up?" he asked after a brief pause.

Ritika gasped but quickly composed herself.

"Rohan," she snapped again.

I found it fascinating how he managed to disappoint me every time he opened his mouth.

"And how exactly do you know her?" I asked curiously.

"Ritika, of course," he winked.

"Okay," I said obnoxiously, looking at Ritika. She shrugged.

"And besides, who does not know about the famous Madhav and his girlfriend Kuhi," he chuckled.

"She is not my girlfriend," I snapped.

"ROHAN," Ritika scowled.

"Oh, come on, Ritika," he said and brushed her cheek with his finger. "I was only trying to lighten the mood here."

I looked at Ritika, giving her a look of sheer disapproval. They were like two opposite poles—she was sensible and smart, while he was brash and childish. Had I not witnessed it for myself, I would have never believed that Ritika could date someone like him.

"Let us order, please," she said. "I am starving."

"So am I," Rohan said.

"I am not hungry," I said.

"Someone has other plans for the evening, it seems," Rohan grinned.

Toes digging into my shoes and fists clenched, I still smiled formally at him.

I was getting annoyed by his demeanour and his stupid banter.

"Ritika, I think I shall go," I said.

"My head feels a little heavy… I need some rest."

Ritika nodded, realising it was best not to stop me.

"Okay then," she said. "See you tomorrow."

I nodded and stood up.

"Nice meeting you, man," Rohan said, his teeth gleaming in the light.

"Take care, and yes, take care of Kuhi as well."

I nodded.

As I was getting up from my chair, I heard him say,

"It must have been quite devastating for her… not to mention the illness of course. Poor girl."

"Ritika, what is he saying?" I gazed at Ritika, turning back.

"Madhav," she said, her voice trembling.

"He does not know about it?" Rohan asked Ritika.

She did not say anything.

"Ritika, what's wrong?" I said, growing impatient with each passing moment.

"Okay," finally, she spoke. "I wanted to tell you, but one thing led to another and…"

"Get to the point," I snapped.

"Kuhi lost her father," she sighed.

"What?" I said.

For a moment, I thought I had misheard what she said.

"WHAT?" I said again, this time loud enough for everyone else to hear.

Rohan shifted his gaze swiftly from Ritika to me.

Ritika nodded and looked down.

"Yes," she said.

Surely, that could not have been true. Perhaps they were only joking, but it was a distasteful joke by even Rohan's petty standards, and Ritika would never do that.

"Why did you not tell me?" I stuttered.

"When?"

"Why did she not tell me?"

"Did you give her a chance to speak?" Ritika said, almost teary-eyed.

"You never gave either Kuhi or me any chance to speak. Therefore, I brought you here, so that I could tell you, but again you never wanted to listen. You kept on repeating that she was only ill, and she should have been reasonable, but Madhav, she was surely not just ill. She had gone through a lot, and I hate to break it to you, but perhaps she suffered the same trauma as you, if not more."

I stood there not knowing how to react. I felt the guilt of the entire world pour down upon me. This time, tears trickled down my cheeks, and I had formed a lump in my throat, making any effort to speak futile.

I sat down on the chair because I felt the ground below me shake violently.

"Madhav," she said, placing both of her hands over mine. "You need to be with her."

"She is one of the strongest women I have ever seen. She decided to act as if nothing had happened to support you, but you never gave her a chance."

"She needs you; go make amends before it is too late."

I sat there trying to absorb everything that had transpired in the past few minutes.

I realised I had committed a grave mistake, and I was cursing myself. I knew I had to do something about it, and I jolted out of the place and rang Kuhi.

No, she did not pick up the phone. I kept calling her, but she did not respond.

I sent her a hundred texts pleading for forgiveness, but she wouldn't reply to my messages either.

My insides lurched, and my heart sank. I knew my one mistake was going to cost me dearly, and I wanted desperately to undo it.

I called her again and stood for hours outside her hostel, hoping to find her, but with no luck.

Finding none, I returned to my room with swollen eyes.

"Are you okay?" Prachurjya asked, standing outside my room just before dinner.

"You haven't changed clothes either."

"Come inside," I said in a hushed tone.

He came in and sat next to me.

"Ritika told me everything," he said, placing his hand on my shoulder.

I didn't look at him and rested my face in my hands.

"Look, it will be alright," he said, in a very *'unlike Prachurjya'* tone.

"I wonder if she will ever talk to me again. What I did was wrong, very wrong," I said.

"She will," he smiled.

"Trust me. Life goes on, bro. Give it some time."

"Now, freshen up. Let's go eat something and get some rest. We will see what we can do about it tomorrow."

I nodded. He stood up and walked towards the door.

"Prachurjya," I said quietly.

"Yes?" he replied.

"Do you mind if I borrow a cigarette?" I asked, feeling slightly embarrassed.

He smiled and nodded, clearly amused.

"Just one… Don't tell Ritika, or she will kill us both," he said with a grin.

I laughed as he lit the cigarette.

He took a couple of puffs and then passed it to me.

"First time, right?" he asked.

I nodded.

"Take it easy, then," he chuckled.

As I took my first few puffs, I was struck by a strange aftertaste and appalled by how bad it tasted.

"So, how is Ritika's boyfriend?" he asked while finishing off the cigarette.

"Oh, you wouldn't want to know, trust me," I replied, shaking my head in distress.

"What a mess."

"Ritika's boyfriend, after all," Prachurjya said, and we both shared a laugh at his remark.

"True," I said as we strolled down towards the dining hall together.

Chapter 24

A GLIMMER OF HOPE

DAY 17: Another day without you, and the disbelief still lingers. We were meant to be together, so why this distance? You always smelled like home, yet now I feel lost, adrift. The pain is insufferable, beyond words. You were the gentle raindrop that kissed me goodbye, and the firefly that guided me home. But now, you are not here anymore, and nothing seems fine. I miss you so much, Kuhi, and all I hope for is your forgiveness—maybe just one last time.

I suddenly stopped typing, as my thumb wavered between the '*send*' and the '*backspace*' key. It had been seventeen days since our last contact, and the pain was overwhelming. I stared at the message I had just typed and scrolled through the hundred other messages I had sent, hoping for a text back from her.

Nothing. Again.

For the past few days, unlocking and locking my phone had become a ritual, driven by the faint hope that she might reach out.

I tried speaking to her after her classes, called her a million times, flooded her inbox, even wrote her emails, but nothing worked. Maybe she was hurt, perhaps hurt in more ways than I could fathom. But I was sorry, genuinely sorry, and would have done anything to have her back.

I dropped my phone onto the bed and lit a cigarette, pulling in the dense smoke. I had started carrying packets of these in my bag, and they had become my crutch— each puff a reminder of my own helplessness, as if she had already walked away for good. Ritika wasn't speaking to me anymore, angry that I had taken to smoking. She had warned me, pleaded even, but I would not stop.

Most days, I spent holed up in my room, surrounded by smoke and thoughts I could not escape. The cigarettes helped dull the ache in my chest, though occasionally, I would feel my chest get heavier. I brushed it off, thinking it was from the pain of losing Kuhi. When the pain came, I would light up another. I ignored calls, saw less of Prachurjya, and distanced myself from everyone who cared. My life had spiralled out of control, and I was too numb to care.

My phone was filled with unread messages, friends asking if I was okay. Ritika had stopped texting after countless unanswered messages. In class, we barely exchanged words. I had shut everyone out—except Kuhi. I left her chat window open, but she was never online. She hadn't blocked me; I figured she had deleted her account.

I flicked the cigarette butt out of the window and lay back on my bed. The fan overhead spun lazily, and the room felt suffocating, its walls closing in on me, echoing one name: Kuhi.

Not long ago, I had won the cup for our hostel, and Kuhi had gone out for coffee with me. Not long ago, I had given her the best birthday surprise I could think of. Back then, I thought I was hers, and she was mine. But now, none of it mattered—not to her, at least.

My mother always told me that life could change in the blink of an eye.

"Stop asking for reasons and always stay prepared," she would say. She was right. Life had changed, and I hadn't seen it coming. I wasn't prepared. How could I be? Kuhi meant everything to me, and no amount of time could have prepared me for this loss.

Just as I was about to light another cigarette, my phone beeped. I almost ignored it; certain it was another pointless notification. But when I checked it, my hands froze, and the cigarette fell from my mouth because I smiled the widest, I could remember.

"Meet me at Niribili at 6:15 tomorrow morning. We need to talk."

Kuhi had finally texted, and tears welled up as a smile broke across my face. Relief washed over me like a wave. Before I could type out a reply, another message came through: *"But don't bother coming if you light another cigarette."*

I chuckled through my tears, staring at the cigarette packet on my desk. With a final smile, I lit it and took one last puff before discarding the cigarette and the packet into the trash. Nothing mattered more than Kuhi, not in that moment, and nothing ever would.

For the first time in weeks, I didn't smoke for hours, resisting the wildest temptation. Even though the craving clawed at me, I held on. The fear of losing her again outweighed any withdrawal I felt. I knew that if she walked away again, there would be no coming back. In fact, I wasn't sure she had come back yet, but just knowing that things might work out gave me hope.

That night, I could hardly sleep. I kept playing out scenarios in my head—how I would greet her, how I would finally pour my heart out, how I would apologise, hold her close, and tell her everything I had been holding back. Most of all, I wanted to make sure I never lost her again.

When I finally drifted off, I entered a strange dream. I found myself sitting on a bench at Niribili, the same place where Kuhi had asked me to meet her. A girl in a white dress sat next to me, her face turned away. She spoke, and her voice sounded familiar, but I couldn't place it. As I leaned closer, the voice became clearer—Kuhi's. But when she finally turned toward me, it wasn't her at all. It was Ritika, speaking in Kuhi's voice. I couldn't make sense of it. Just as I was about to say something, my alarm beeped, jolting me awake.

The dream left me unsettled and groggy, but I brushed it off. I had more important things on my mind. I put on my joggers, determined to be at the park early, and rushed out the door.

To my surprise, when I arrived, Kuhi was already there, and it looked like she had been waiting for a while.

Chapter 25

MY GIRL IN ALL SHADES

There she was, sitting on the bench, her hair tied back in a ponytail. It had grown longer since the first time I saw her, from just brushing her shoulders to now reaching halfway down her back. The red-dyed tips that once complemented her bright face had faded with time. I stood still for a moment, wondering if she even noticed me. This was the first time we would speak in eighteen days—the longest we had ever gone without talking. Those eighteen days had been some of the hardest of my life, and I wondered if they had been just as difficult for her.

"Hi," I said, my voice tight with tension.

She looked up and smiled, though it was tinged with an awkwardness that mirrored mine.

"Hi," she said softly.

"Come here, sit," she said, rubbing the space on the bench beside her.

I sat down on the old bench, releasing a breath I hadn't realized I was holding. A few moments passed in silence before I finally gathered the courage to speak.

"How have you been?" I asked.

She turned towards me, her smile faltering.

"Same as I was the last time we spoke," she replied, her eyes misty.

Guilt washed over me—a guilt I wanted to address but didn't quite know how to.

"Why haven't you shaved?" she asked, rubbing her eyes.

I shrugged, unsure of how to respond.

"And your lips," she sighed.

"They are so dark now. I never imagined that Madhav, who was always so conscious about his health and fitness, would start smoking."

I licked my lips instinctively, as if that would somehow change their colour and hide the evidence of my habit.

"I know, it surprises me too. It's... it's just been so hard. Everything felt like it was slipping away. Smoking... I don't know. It was like a way to fill the void when you weren't there. A distraction, I guess," I said.

She furrowed her brow, concern clouding her face.

"But that's not you. Smoking, hurting yourself like this—Madhav, it's not you," she said.

I sighed.

"You are right. It's not me, but I guess I was just trying to feel something other than... perpetual loss. I was angry— at myself, at the situation, at you—even though I knew it wasn't fair. Smoking was just a way to escape that feeling for a moment. But in the end, it just made everything worse."

"You don't need that, Madhav. I am with you. And I don't want to lose you to this... I don't want to see you destroy yourself because of me," she said.

Her words echoed in my mind, wrapping themselves around my heart. I had been so focused on numbing my pain that I hadn't considered how it might affect her to see me like this.

Tears welled up in my eyes. I was teetering on the edge of breaking down. She reached out and held both my hands, offering the comfort I so desperately needed.

"I am sorry," she whispered. "I shouldn't have done what I did."

"Shhh," I said, placing my fingers on her lips.

"It wasn't your fault. I was so caught up in complaining about my own pain that I didn't even stop to think that you might have been suffering too. I acted like my problems were the only ones that mattered. I was selfish; I have always been a little selfish."

"No, you are not," she said, but she didn't sound as convincing as she usually did. Perhaps a part of her agreed with what I had said.

"I am sorry, Kuhi. I really am. But believe me, I had no idea what you were going through."

She clutched my hand as if to comfort me.

Her touch made everything else melt away, all the pain and confusion dissolving in that moment.

"You know," I said, "I didn't realise how hard it would be to live without you until you were gone. The last eighteen days have been the worst of my life, and I never want to go through that again. Please, don't let go of me again."

She smiled at me—the sweetest, most comforting smile I had seen in what felt like a lifetime. She nodded and tapped my shoulder gently.

"Never," she whispered. "Not in a thousand years."

I pulled her close, holding her tightly. In the silence that followed, the only sound was our breathing—a rhythm that somehow felt familiar, like coming home.

"You know something?" I said softly. She shook her head, blinking.

"I thought I had lost you," I stuttered, barely able to get the words out. "I thought I had lost you for good, and it was the worst feeling in the world—suffocating, painful, crippling."

"I could run out of words trying to explain how much it hurt, Kuhi. It was unbearable, like nothing I have ever felt before."

She tightened her grip on my hand, her touch like a lifeline I hadn't realised I was clinging to.

"Everything happens for a reason," she said quietly, brushing her hand across my face.

"I don't understand," I replied, confused.

She shifted in her seat, placing her hand back over mine.

"If none of this had happened, we wouldn't be here right now, on this bench, having this conversation. Sometimes we take people for granted, assuming they will always be there, but we never really know what the next moment might bring."

I gazed into her eyes, unblinking, absorbing every word.

"My dad..." she began, her voice faltering as she choked on her words. She took a deep breath, rubbing the tears from her cheeks. This time, I held her hand tighter, gently resting my forehead against hers.

"My dad was with me when I was in the hospital, fighting dengue. He would take care of me, make sure I took my medicines, and watch over me while I slept—at least, he thought I was asleep. But then one day, while I was still in the hospital, he had a cardiac arrest."

She burst into tears, and I couldn't hold mine back either. I wrapped my arms around her as she sobbed into my shoulder.

"He was alone at home, Madhav. We didn't even know. We only found out when he didn't answer our calls. We rushed him to the hospital, but... it was too late. I lost him. I lost my dad." Her tears flowed like torrential rain—endless and devastating.

"I couldn't even say goodbye."

I wanted to say something, anything to comfort her, but fell short of words. Before I could figure it out, she spoke again.

"But that's life, isn't it?" she said, covering her tears with a fragile smile. "I have learnt that nothing lasts forever. The only constant is that everything will eventually end. So, while we are here, we should cherish every moment, live it fully."

I looked at her, my heart swelling with admiration. Kuhi was indeed the strongest person I knew, just as Ritika had pointed out, and I was grateful she was with me.

"I love you," I said, the words tumbling out before I could stop them. I realised then, with absolute certainty, that she was the one person I couldn't live without.

For a moment, she stood speechless, her eyes wide with surprise. Then she smiled, tears of joy glistening in her eyes.

"I love you too, Madhav. And I mean it," she whispered, her voice full of emotion.

"Please don't break my heart."

"Never in a million years," I said and leaned in for a kiss.

She did not hesitate.

In that moment, it felt like everything had finally fallen into place. The girl I had dreamt of being with was finally mine, and I couldn't imagine anything more perfect.

And in that moment, I realised she wasn't just *The Girl in White*—she was *My Girl* in all her shades, every hue of pain and joy, and I loved every bit of her.

Chapter 26

OUR MOMENT IN TIME

"Just one more spoon, come on... Hurry up," Kuhi said, her eyes gleaming as she tried to shove another spoonful of oats into my mouth.

"No, no... put that away," I protested, leaning back.

"Do you love me?" she asked, raising her eyebrows mischievously.

"Of course," I said, and the moment I opened my mouth, she, with cat-like quickness, drove the spoon inside. I had no choice but to gulp it down.

"That is so unfair!" I groaned.

She laughed and playfully pulled the tip of my nose.

We were sitting in the cafeteria after classes, and she had prepared oatmeal for me, determined to feed me every last grain from the tiffin.

"Do you realise how much weight you have lost?" she said, her expression softening.

I shrugged, unsure of what else to say.

"So, keep your tantrums to yourself and eat up," she commanded, her tone playful but firm.

I mimicked her stern expression, and we both burst into laughter.

"And if I ever see you with another cigarette," she added, "I swear I am going to suck the soul out of you."

I raised an eyebrow, smirking. "Only if it were something else instead of my soul."

"*Ewww!*" she laughed, smacking my arm. "Your dirty little mind..."

"Now come on, finish this," she said, shaking her head.

"We don't have all day."

I blew her a kiss and nodded, pretending to give in. She raised her eyebrows but blew a kiss back.

The world suddenly seemed wonderful again. Kuhi was mine, and I couldn't imagine her being anywhere else. I had finally found the happiness I had been searching for. Despite all the pain we had both gone through, we had each other again. She was my home.

As I begrudgingly finished the last spoonful, I couldn't help but smile at the way she fussed over me.

Suddenly Kuhi glanced at her watch and nudged me.

"We should get going. Ritika is going to be furious if we make her wait any longer."

Just as I was about to protest, a familiar voice cut through the chatter around us.

"Still not done, both of you?" Ritika's voice came from behind, her arms crossed, smirking.

"Lovebirds… no wonder."

"Rohan and you, you mean," I teased, nudging Kuhi with a smirk.

Ritika narrowed her eyes at me, her lips curling into a warning smile.

"Careful, Madhav," she shot back. "You are not half as funny as you think."

I chuckled but threw up my hands in mock surrender.

"Alright, alright. No need to get violent," I said, leaning into Kuhi like she was my shield.

"Besides, I wouldn't want to get in the middle of your romantic comedy."

"Let's go!" she said impatiently. "We are already late."

We had planned an outing together, and Rohan—Ritika's new boyfriend—was supposed to join us too. It was apparently a *double movie date.* Despite my strong reservations about going out with Rohan, Kuhi insisted it would be a good opportunity for us to get to know each other better.

"Is Prachurjya not joining us?" Kuhi asked.

"No," I said coolly.

Ritika gave me a concerned look. I avoided her gaze, but before Kuhi could ask anything else, Ritika called out again, "Come on! The bus isn't going to wait forever."

I chuckled. "Do you know why Ritika loves the university bus so much?" I asked, teasingly.

"Don't even start!" Ritika warned.

"Oh, but she should know!" I laughed.

Ritika rushed towards me, threatening a punch. "I swear, Madhav, don't you dare!"

Before she could hit me, Kuhi whispered, "Ouch."

Both Ritika and I froze and looked at her, only to burst into laughter.

"You two are insane," Kuhi said, shaking her head in disbelief.

"We know," we said in unison.

"You know, your mister thinks he is a bit of a spy," Ritika said to Kuhi, smirking.

"What?" Kuhi and I both said, confused.

"Don't you remember, Madhav?" Ritika continued, her smirk widening. "That day when we came to the theatre for a movie. You were texting Kuhi, acting all secretive, thinking I didn't notice."

My face burned with embarrassment as Kuhi started giggling.

"I knew he liked you from day one," Ritika teased, "but that day it became obvious. Glad you don't have to play *James Bond* anymore, right?"

"I am glad you don't have to play *Sherlock*," I interjected, trying to regain some composure.

Kuhi laughed harder, while Ritika shot me a mock glare, but I could tell she was holding back a smile.

Soon after, Ritika introduced Kuhi to Rohan, who had joined us. He gave me a slight nod of acknowledgment, and I did the same. For some reason, we never really got along despite Ritika's best efforts. We had four premium tickets, giving us four large recliners right at the back. Kuhi and I took the front two while Ritika and Rohan sat behind us.

For the first quarter of an hour, we both watched the movie in silence, though I could feel the electricity between us. Her arm brushed mine every now and then, sending ripples through my skin. I didn't dare move, worried that if I shifted even slightly, I would break the spell.

Then, slowly—almost hesitantly—Kuhi leaned closer, her head finally resting against my shoulder. My breath caught in my throat. This was something I had imagined for so long. Every stolen glance, every laugh we shared, all leading to this one quiet, perfect moment. I could feel her warmth seep into me, the soft strands of her hair brushing against my neck. I always dreamt of going to the movies with her, holding her close like this. And now, it was finally happening.

I looked at her, and she met my gaze. Her eyes spoke volumes, and I got lost in them—those eyes that held infinity, an endless depth of love that I never wanted to let go of.

They say, *"You may move on from someone you loved, but the eyes that captured your heart stay with you."* At that moment, I understood exactly what it meant. Even if there ever came a day when Kuhi wasn't by my side, the love in those eyes would stay with me forever.

"Kuhi," I whispered, gently running my fingers through her hair. She smiled but quickly buried her face in my shoulder, her breathing becoming uneven. Moments later, she began to sob, her voice muffled as she tried to suppress her cries.

I knew what was happening. The pain of her father's demise was still fresh, a wound that hadn't healed.

I could feel the heavy, unspoken weight of her grief as Kuhi's sobs grew more intense. The warmth of her body pressed against mine, the way her tears soaked into my shirt, all spoke of a pain that was deep and unyielding.

Ritika glanced our way, but I signalled that everything was okay.

"Madhav," Kuhi choked out, her voice breaking through the tears. "I really... I loved him. I wish I had just one more moment to tell him what he meant to me. Just one last minute with him... I miss him so much."

Her sobs were like a raw, unfiltered expression of her heartache. I held her tighter, my embrace a silent promise of support. I didn't need words; I just needed to be there, sharing in her grief and offering what solace I could.

When she finally paused, her breath still shaky, I tilted her chin gently, forcing myself to meet her tear-streaked eyes.

"Kuhi, no one can truly understand the depth of your loss, and nothing can replace the love you had for him. But

I am here for you—today, tomorrow, and always. I would go to any lengths for you. You are mine, and I promise to be by your side forever. I love you."

Her embrace tightened around me, as though she was holding on for dear life.

"I love you too, Madhav," she whispered, her voice trembling. "I can't afford to lose you. Not again. If I do, I won't know what to do, I'll be gone... far away."

"I can't keep on losing people that matter to me."

I placed a finger gently on her lips, shushing her softly. "*Shhh*, no one will ever come between us. Not now, not ever."

"I'll always be here for you."

In that quiet space, her tear-filled eyes met mine. With a slow, deliberate movement, she leaned in, and our lips touched. The kiss was tender, filled with raw emotion, the salty taste of her tears a reminder of the depth of her feelings.

The world outside melted away. We were completely absorbed in our own universe—two souls bound together, finding solace and love in each other. The movie, the people around us, even Ritika's deliberate coughing, all faded into the background. It was just us, my *Girl in White*, and the profound moment of our shared love.

Chapter 27

THE CALM BEFORE THE STORM?

"They look so happy together, don't they?" Kuhi said as we made our way back.

We had managed to find a seat on the bus. She was sitting by the window, and her hair kept brushing against my face. At times, she would rest her head on my chest, quiet and still, and other times, she would chatter non-stop, making it hard for me to keep up.

It had become dark outside, and though we were all a bit drowsy, Kuhi's radiant charm made me want to keep staring at her.

"I suppose," I shrugged.

"Why don't you like Rohan?" she asked with a giggle. "He seems like a nice guy to me."

"I never said I don't like him," I replied, trying to steer the conversation away. "Besides, he is Ritika's boyfriend, so there is no reason for me not to like him."

"That's what I am asking," she said, raising an eyebrow. "Is it Rohan himself you don't like, or just that he is with Ritika?"

I looked taken aback.

"Kuhi," I said, slightly annoyed.

"Sorry," she laughed, giving me a playful poke in the ribs.

"Ouch," I said, pretending to be hurt. "You—"

I grabbed her hand and began tickling her until we realised the other passengers on the bus were staring at us.

"Looks like that oatmeal is starting to give you some extra energy," she teased, her eyes sparkling with mischief. "You are practically a tickling champion now!"

I threw her a look of mock disdain.

She sighed.

"Okay, okay," she said once people stopped looking at us. "So, is everything okay between Prachurjya and you?"

"Yes," I said, though my voice betrayed a hint of doubt.

Kuhi kept looking at me.

I looked away, feeling uneasy. Prachurjya had been acting strangely lately, and I suspected it was because he felt left out. I had invited him to the movie, but he declined.

"I don't know," I finally admitted. "I think he feels a bit excluded now that Ritika and I have company."

She nodded thoughtfully.

"Hey, why don't we ask him to accompany us for lunch tomorrow?"

Her eyes sparkled with enthusiasm.

"I am not sure that is a good idea," I said.

"But then again, I don't want Prachurjya to feel left out, so I suppose we could give it a try."

"Perfect!" she beamed. "Just bring him to '*The Three Chefs*' tomorrow, and he will be fine."

I hesitated, but her excitement was infectious. I agreed to her plan, even though I had a bad feeling about it.

"So, what's the plan?" I asked.

"That's a secret," she winked.

"You will see."

I studied her for a moment before speaking. "Kuhi, I know you want to help, but sometimes what Prachurjya might need is not forced company. He might just need some space."

"Everyone needs company, Madhav," she countered. "Don't worry, just be there on time tomorrow."

I nodded.

When the bus finally stopped, I dropped Kuhi off at her hostel and headed back to mine.

On the way, I saw Anuj and Jayanta practising on the field for the university's tour to West Bengal from a distance. I could feel my insides lurch, wishing to be on the field too. But deep down, I was also grateful to be on my feet. If it weren't for the recent events, I might not have been with Kuhi.

"The Butterfly Effect!" I mumbled and walked on.

Once I reached the hostel, I tried calling Prachurjya, but he didn't answer. After several rings, he finally picked up.

"Busy?" I asked.

"Not really," he replied sceptically. "I was just looking for my lighter."

"Found it, then?" I inquired.

"Why did you call?" he asked.

"Dude, what is going on?" I asked, sensing his mood.

"Get to the point, Madhav," he said flatly. "If it's not important, I'll call you back later. I have things to do."

His tone annoyed me, but I kept my composure.

"Prachurjya, you are more than just a friend. If something is bothering you, you can tell me."

"Am I?" he said rhetorically.

"Thanks, but I am fine," he said.

"Okay," I sighed.

"Listen, Kuhi wants to meet you at *'The Three Chefs'* tomorrow."

"She wants to?" he replied sarcastically.

"She wants to have lunch with you," I said, frustration mounting.

"I am a bit busy tomorrow. I won't be able to make it," he said.

"Stop being a jerk!" I raised my voice.

"You don't need to lecture me," he snapped.

"Seriously? I am trying to help you!" I shot back, exasperated.

"Fine, I'll just tell her you are not coming."

As I was about to disconnect the call, he interjected.

"No, wait..." his voice softened, almost regretful.

"I am sorry, man. It has just been... a rough day."

"I'll come."

"Great! Thanks," I said and disconnected the call.

I was annoyed, but I didn't let it show. I called Kuhi to let her know he would come but warned her to be careful since Prachurjya wasn't his usual self.

She assured me, saying she knew what she was doing and that Prachurjya would appreciate it.

That evening, we didn't talk much. Kuhi was tired, and I got busy with some classwork.

Later, I went for a walk alone. The streets were filled with cheerful groups, and their laughter reminded me of the days when Prachurjya and I used to be inseparable. We would wander around these very roads, talking about everything from our dreams to the most random things. Back then, it was so easy between us—no awkward silences, no hidden tension.

But now, something has changed. Was it me? Had I been too wrapped up in my own life—with Kuhi, with Ritika? I couldn't help but wonder if I had pushed him away without even realising it. The thought gnawed at me.

Kuhi's plan might help, but I couldn't shake the feeling that it wouldn't be enough. Prachurjya wasn't someone who could just be 'fixed' with lunch. He was proud, and sometimes I think he just wanted to be left alone. But I couldn't leave him like this. Not when it felt like I was losing my closest friend.

"Madhav!" someone called from behind. It was Anuj. We hadn't been in touch much lately; he had been busy preparing for the West Bengal tournament while I was recovering from my injury.

"Hi Anuj," I greeted with a smile.

"How's the preparation going?" I asked.

"Trying," he said. "The Inter-University didn't go as planned. Losing a key player like you and getting knocked out in the first round was tough. I hope West Bengal will be kinder to us. Plus, the fact that this will officially be my last tournament in university colours makes it even more special to me."

"Don't worry," I said. "You will do great."

"I hope so," he sighed. "How is your recovery?"

"Better than when you first saw me with the injury," I laughed.

He smiled. "Recover soon, champ."

"The team needs you."

"Hopefully soon," I said, returning the smile.

He nodded and walked away.

"How will Prachurjya react tomorrow?" I wondered to myself. "Will he be happy? Embarrassed? What will he think of Kuhi's mysterious plan?"

My phone rang, breaking the silence of my thoughts. "*Maa*," the screen read. I paused for a moment before answering, feeling a sudden sense of relief wash over me.

"Hello," I said, trying to sound composed.

"*Rubu, ki korisa?*" (Rubu, what are you doing?) Her familiar voice was warm, like a gentle hug after a long, exhausting day.

I hadn't realised how tense I had been until that moment. The weight of everything—Prachurjya, Kuhi, the uncertainty about the next day—seemed to ease just by hearing her. It was strange how she always had that effect, no matter how far I was or how much I had on my mind.

"*Asu anei, Maa*" (Nothing much, Maa), I replied, a smile tugging at my lips. For a moment, all the noise inside my head quieted. She didn't need to know about my worries, my doubts. Just hearing her was enough to remind me that, no matter how chaotic life got, some things—like her love—were constant.

"Take care of yourself, Rubu," she said softly, and it felt like everything would be okay, at least for then.

As we said our goodbyes, I felt grounded again. The anxiety from earlier didn't vanish, but it was easier to bear. Mothers—they have a way of making even the toughest days feel a little lighter.

Chapter 28

THE ARRIVAL OF WINTER

I arrived at the location well ahead of the scheduled time, but to my surprise, Kuhi was nowhere to be found. She had told me she was already there, yet neither she nor Prachurjya was in sight. I wondered if I had come too early or if I was even at the right place. I dialled Kuhi's number, but she didn't pick up. Checking my watch, I saw it was twelve forty-five.

As I scanned the area, I noticed a couple of familiar faces from the university, but none that I really knew well.

I started to wonder if they were pulling a prank. Just as I was about to call Kuhi again, I felt a tap on my shoulder.

"Looking for someone?" a familiar voice giggled behind me.

I turned around to see Divya, one of Kuhi's close friends. Divya and Kuhi had been classmates and friends since their first day at the university.

"Hi," I said, taken aback.

"Ah, talking to me, but your eyes are clearly searching for someone else," she teased with a knowing smile.

I chuckled, embarrassed. "Have you seen Kuhi?"

"Look behind," she said with a smirk.

I turned, and there she was—Kuhi, wearing a black kurti with a yellow dupatta, looking stunning.

"Finally!" I sighed. "Where were you?"

"In your mind," Divya interrupted.

Kuhi giggled, and I just shook my head.

"That was terrible," I said.

"As if you crack decent jokes… Kuhi tells me about all your silly, unfunny jokes," Divya shot back.

"I did not use the word '*unfunny*'," Kuhi chimed in, her face turning pink.

"Unbelievable," I sighed.

"Anyway, what's the plan?" I asked, trying to regain some composure.

"The plan is standing right next to you," Kuhi replied, stifling a giggle.

"Eh? What?" I blinked, confused, as both Divya and Kuhi burst into laughter.

I had no idea what was happening, so I stood there, waiting for them to have their moment. Once they finally calmed down, Kuhi began to explain the situation. She told me how Divya had fancied Prachurjya since our first class—much like how I had taken a liking to Kuhi. Today, the plan was to bring them together.

Divya was from Uttarakhand. She had long, jet-black hair tied in a loose braid most of the time and was wearing a lavender salwar kameez that day. She also liked poetry, a trait that was quite opposite to Prachurjya. I wasn't sure if Prachurjya felt the same about her, but I decided not to address it.

"Are you sure this is the right time or place?" I asked.

"Yes," said Kuhi with resounding confidence.

"Okay," I nodded, though not entirely convinced.

"So why isn't he here yet?" Divya asked.

"Probably tied up with something," I said, trying to sound nonchalant. "He should be here soon."

"Alright then, let's find a table for four," Kuhi beamed.

As we sat, Kuhi insisted that I sit next to Divya, claiming that Prachurjya should face her for "maximum effect."

"Whatever you say, but if things go south, don't blame me," I said.

"Whatever," Kuhi replied, trying to ignore my remark.

"Don't worry, I'll manage," Divya said with a wide smile.

"Someone cannot stop smiling," Kuhi added, and the two burst into laughter.

Although I wasn't entirely convinced by Kuhi's plan, I was at least content with the possibility that, if it succeeded, I would have to go out with Prachurjya and Divya instead of Rohan for a future *'double movie date'*.

I was just settling in when Kuhi's voice lit up. "Hey, look! There's Prachurjya."

We all turned to see him entering the hall, flicking a cigarette outside before walking in.

Kuhi waved, and he nodded in acknowledgment.

When he joined us, Kuhi wasted no time making introductions. "Prachurjya, meet Divya—my classmate and a dear friend."

Prachurjya's greeting was lukewarm at best. His eyes barely glanced at Divya before darting away, and his fingers drummed impatiently on the table. I could sense the tension simmering beneath his indifferent expression—something wasn't right.

Kuhi, sensing the growing awkwardness, jumped into conversation, trying to break the ice, but Prachurjya's cold, one-word replies only deepened the unease. His irritation was palpable, like a storm cloud looming overhead, ready to burst at any moment.

"Prachurjya, there is something we wanted to talk about," Kuhi finally said.

I shot her a worried glance.

"Yes," Prachurjya replied, looking a bit confused.

Kuhi took a deep breath and continued, "We have all noticed that something has been bothering you lately."

"We just want to help, and we think maybe you need someone special in your life. Someone who understands you," she said in a compassionate tone.

His expression remained unreadable as he listened. I grew more uneasy with each passing second, fearing this calm exterior masked something deeper.

Kuhi continued, "Someone you can talk to, someone who can be there for you in ways we can't. In the end, we all need someone, don't we?"

"Madhav is also occupied mostly, and I know being lonely can be excruciating sometimes," she added.

For the first time, I saw Prachurjya's jaw tighten. His silence was starting to feel ominous, like the calm before a storm.

"I only want the best for you, for you to smile and be happy so that we can all be happy again… together."

"We thought Divya could be that person," Kuhi said hopefully, gesturing toward her friend.

That was the breaking point.

"So that's why I am here," Prachurjya said, exhaling loudly. "You are playing '*Matchmaker*' then?"

"Prachurjya, no—" Kuhi began, but he cut her off, his voice rising.

"No, Kuhi, you need to listen to me," he snapped, his voice rising enough to draw the attention of nearby tables.

"I don't need anyone deciding what is best for me. I don't need your interference."

My fists clenched at his words, and I wanted to jump in, but he wasn't finished.

"I can make my own decisions. And Divya, you—" he said, turning toward her with a sarcastic smile. "I never knew you were this desperate."

"They were right about you. You are nothing but desperate and clingy."

"Forget me; no one would want to come close to you."

Divya let out a gasp, and tears rolled down her cheeks.

Kuhi's face turned pale, her eyes brimming with tears. The situation had spiralled out of control.

"You don't need to teach me to be happy. As a matter of fact, you don't need to tell me who I should be with and who I shouldn't be with, Kuhi."

"You came between our group and spoiled everything. We were happy before you showed up and you started behaving like you belong."

"You don't," he continued, releasing all his pent-up frustration. "I wish you never came back here after your petty illness."

I couldn't hold back anymore.

"Who the hell do you think you are?" I shouted, standing up, fists still tight.

"How dare you talk to her like that? All she ever wanted was to help you, to make sure you are happy. But you are too self-absorbed to see that."

Prachurjya sneered, clearly unfazed, before storming out.

Divya, devastated, excused herself to the washroom, while Kuhi sat there, puzzled, not knowing what had happened.

"Kuhi," I said.

She didn't answer.

She then stood up and left.

I hurried after her, my heart pounding, anger still boiling over.

I was ashamed to call Prachurjya my friend. Everything had unravelled so fast, and I wasn't sure how to fix any of it. Watching Kuhi walk away, tears threatening to spill over, I realised just how deeply everything had spiralled out of control.

I felt extremely helpless, and I had no idea what to do next.

Chapter 29

CROSSROADS

"Open the door!" I yelled, pounding on Prachurjya's room with all my might.

"Go away, Madhav," came his muffled voice from inside.

My anger was fuelling up, and my need for answers was unwavering. I was not going to walk away without understanding why he had done what he did.

"Prachurjya, open the damn door," I shouted, slamming it again.

"Because I felt like it," he replied curtly.

That wasn't good enough.

"Prachurjya, I am asking you once again… open the door," I pleaded, my frustration rising.

"Go away," he roared.

There was a long pause, and then the door creaked open. He stepped out and brushed past me, his face expressionless. I stared at him, struggling to recognise the friend I once knew.

"I want an explanation," I said, trying to keep my voice steady.

"I don't owe you or your *'girlfriend'* anything, least of all, an explanation," he said, not looking back.

I did not know what happened, but I just snapped. Perhaps it was the frustration brewing inside, but I lost my composure. My hand shot out, grabbing his collar before I could even think. Rage clouded my vision, and all I could see was red. "Don't you ever… in your miserable life… disrespect Kuhi again," I growled.

His face turned purple as I tightened my grip. "Madhav… let go," he choked out, struggling for air. My rage made me deaf to his pleas.

"Never," I said through clenched teeth. "Never disrespect Kuhi again."

I shoved him against the wall, and he slumped to the floor, gasping for breath. For a moment, I considered helping him, but the anger was too strong. I turned and walked out; my conscience weighed down, but my resolve remained firm.

I felt bad, wanted to go back and tend to him, perhaps hug him, but I did not look back.

Days passed, and the rift between Prachurjya and me remained. We no longer talked with each other. Each time we saw each other, we would change ways. We went from being best friends to strangers.

Once, I even walked up to him to apologise and make things right, but he walked away as soon as he saw me.

Ritika, sensing the tension between us, tried to mediate.

"He is still a kid, Madhav. Try to understand," she said, focused on her assignment. "Let him be. Just forget about it."

"No," I sighed. "He was wrong. Kuhi just wanted to see him happy."

"Besides, I did try and apologise; he walked away like I did not even exist. If he wants it this way, I have no problems with that. I don't mind not having him in my life."

But that was far from the truth. I missed Prachurjya every single day. He had been more than a friend; he was my anchor in this chaotic hostel life, and without him, I felt adrift.

Ritika continued to write, avoiding my gaze. After a moment, she put her pen down and looked at me with a weary expression.

"Madhav, I get that you care about Kuhi. But maybe it's time to let this go."

"You are best friends," she said softly.

"Were," I said.

"Fine, have it your way," she said, returning to her work.

I didn't have a reply. I kept scrolling through my phone, feeling the disconnection. When Ritika finally finished, she looked at me with a smirk.

"Make sure you submit your assignment alongside mine by tomorrow," she said.

I was surprised. "What do you mean?"

"You haven't finished yours, have you?" she teased. "You can copy mine."

Amidst all the chaos, I had completely forgotten about the assignment that was due the next day.

Relief washed over me. Ritika had always been a lifesaver.

"Ritika, what would I truly do without you?" I said, feeling grateful.

"Yeah, whatever," she said.

"Just don't forget to submit it tomorrow," she reminded me.

"Okay," I said. "But why aren't you submitting yours on your own?"

"I am not coming tomorrow," she said, glancing at her phone.

"Why?" I asked, taken aback.

It was very unusual of Ritika to miss classes.

"Rohan is moving to a new flat nearby, and he needs my help moving in," she explained.

I was shocked. Ritika was skipping class to help Rohan move.

"You are kidding, right?" I asked.

"No, Madhav," she said.

"But Ritika…" I started.

"But what, Madhav?" she asked, her voice calm but firm.

"Nothing," I replied, looking down.

"Okay," she said.

After a few moments of silence, I finally mustered the courage to speak again.

"Ritika, can I ask you something?" I said.

"Shoot!" she said.

"Are you really sure about Rohan?" I asked, concern edging my tone.

She looked at me, a mix of irritation and patience in her eyes. "Yes, I am sure."

I nodded, trying to accept her decision. Maybe I was overreacting because I cared about her. We walked back to our hostels, and she mentioned that Rohan was planning something special for her birthday. I had completely forgotten that Ritika's birthday was coming up in less than a week.

"But Ritika," I said.

"Does it ever occur to you that every time Rohan's name comes up, there is always a 'but' involved?" she teased.

"Not funny," I replied.

"Alright, tell me your *'but'*," she insisted.

"I had plans for your birthday too," I admitted, feeling sheepish.

"Really?" she said, her eyes lighting up. "Do you even know when my birthday is?"

"Of course," I said, trying to sound confident. "I have planned a dinner for us."

"Wow," she said with a smile. "That's sweet."

I was relieved she appreciated it, despite my own forgetfulness. "But I don't want to be the reason you bail on Rohan," I said.

Ritika reassured me. "Rohan wouldn't want me to cancel either. He has been looking forward to it for months."

"Ritika," I said, feeling a twinge of worry.

"You please take care of yourself, okay? I don't want you to get hurt, that is all."

She placed her hands on my cheeks and smiled warmly. "Aww… I did not know you were caring too. Don't worry, Mr. Cricketer, I shall be fine."

I nodded, reassured by her words, though Rohan's name still lingered in my thoughts.

Suddenly, Ritika's phone rang, cutting through the silence. She glanced at the screen and stepped away.

"Hang on, it's Rohan."

The ease in our conversation evaporated as quickly as it had come, leaving a tension that buzzed in the space between us.

"So, why did you lie to him about being at the library?" I asked after she was done with the call.

She shrugged. "Just… doesn't have to know everything, does he?"

"Because he might not like you hanging out with me, right?" I said.

"No, Madhav," she said, looking slightly defensive. "It's not like that."

"It is," I insisted. "He dislikes me, and the feeling is mutual."

Ritika remained silent.

"Alright then," I said, feeling a mix of frustration and resignation.

"See you tomorrow in class."

"The day after," she mumbled.

"Right," I sighed.

Chapter 30

FADING SMILES

Kuhi wasn't fine at all. Ever since that encounter at the café, her smile had dimmed, almost as if she had forgotten how to be herself. She had always admired Prachurjya for who he was, but after everything that had unfolded, she could no longer bring herself to talk to him. Even Divya, her best friend, had grown distant. Divya was upset too, though not as much as Kuhi. It came as a shock to all of us, but the person most affected by it was me.

Ever since I had come to this place, Prachurjya had been by my side through thick and thin. He had been my closest companion. Losing that connection with the one person I saw every day was suffocating, as if a part of my daily life was missing.

On the night just before Ritika's birthday, I called her because I wanted to be the first to wish her, but she didn't pick up. Realising she was probably with Rohan, I decided to drop her a text instead.

"Hey, happy birthday :)"

To my surprise, a notification popped up almost immediately.

"Thanks, Madhav. Sorry, couldn't take your call. I'll call you tomorrow. Goodnight."

Something about her quick, polite response felt off, but I tried to shake the feeling. I did not want to disturb her, but at the same time, for some reason, I was starting to feel a little restless.

Everything was starting to fall apart. In a matter of mere months, I had lost the ability to play the sport that meant so much to me, my friendship with Prachurjya had hit rock bottom, my relationship with Kuhi was going through turbulent times, and Ritika, who meant so much to me, was also slowly distancing herself from me.

It felt as though the weight of everything was pressing down on me—my lost game, my fractured friendship, Ritika's growing distance. Dark clouds loomed, threatening to pull me under.

Just then, my phone rang. It was Kuhi.

Seeing her name flash on my screen late at night was jarring. Kuhi was never one for late-night calls, and that alone sent my anxiety skyrocketing.

"Kuhi," I answered, keeping my voice calm. "You haven't slept yet?"

There was a pause before she responded.

"Not yet," she said, her voice heavy with emotion.

"Is something bothering you, Kuhi?" I asked gently. "Hey, what happened?"

"Nothing," she said, but then I heard her sob.

Kuhi had always been the more mature one. Ever since she had come into my life, she had done everything to make sure I didn't feel low. She taught me that no matter how tough things got, we could still smile our way through it. Hearing her break down like this shook me.

"Kuhi," I said softly. "What's wrong, sweetie?"

She didn't reply, but I could hear her trying to hold back her sobs.

"Kuhi, listen to me," I said softly, my heart aching to comfort her. "I am here. I've always been here, and I always will be. I am here for you. Always."

Finally, she spoke, her voice cracking.

"Madhav… I am so sorry," she whispered, her tears choking her words.

"I spoiled everything."

"I miss home."

"I miss my father…"

Before she could finish, she was in tears again. That is when I realised why she was so upset.

Ever since her father had passed, she never really had the chance to mourn her loss apart from that one time at the theatre. She always tried to deflect sorrow, but it was only inevitable that someday it would hit her. Maybe she didn't want to show her sadness at all, choosing instead to support me through my lows. And in doing so, I never shared in her grief, never asked about her pain. I didn't want to bring it up, afraid it would weaken her. But then,

I saw how much she had been holding back, how deeply she was still hurting.

It's hard to recover from losing someone so close, but Kuhi always found a reason to smile. She was strong, but hearing her cry like that broke me.

I stayed quiet, unsure of what to say. I wanted to hold her, to comfort her, but all I had was a phone, and phones can't give you the warmth you need.

It felt like an eternity before she spoke again, her voice a little steadier this time.

"You know, Madhav," she said, "I never wanted to ruin your friendship with Prachurjya. I really didn't."

"It wasn't your fault, Kuhi," I said firmly. "It never was."

"It is my fault," she insisted, her voice cracking again. "If it wasn't for me, maybe Prachurjya would still be your friend."

"Don't ever think that," I said. "I would give up anyone in this world to see you smile."

She didn't reply, but I imagined her nodding through the phone. My anger toward Prachurjya flared up again. The fact that Kuhi was crying because of what he did made me furious.

"All I wanted was for him not to feel left out," she said quietly. "I never thought things would turn out like this. Maybe I should have listened to you…"

I sighed. "Kuhi, don't worry about any of this. Don't lose sleep over it."

There was silence on her end.

"Madhav," she finally said, "talk to him. He is your friend. Maybe he is sorry too but doesn't know how to show it. Will you talk to him? For me?"

"No," I said, my voice firm.

"Please," she said. "Let us all be on good terms again."

"No!" I said again.

"For me?" she repeated, softer this time.

I wanted to refuse, but I finally gave in. I could never say no to her after all.

"Alright," I agreed reluctantly.

"Thank you," she said gently. "Just promise me you won't do anything to make it worse."

I sighed. "I'll try."

Before she hung up, I said, "Kuhi, I'll always be there for you."

"I know… I love you," she whispered, and the call ended.

As I sat there, I realised something. Kuhi was vulnerable, just like all of us, but in her own way. She cared more about others than she did for herself, always pouring her heart into easing their pain while burying her own beneath a smile. That selflessness made her beautiful, but it also made her vulnerable in ways she never let anyone see. But that is what made her who she was.

I had fallen so deeply in love with her that nothing—not Prachurjya, not anyone—could ever change that. She was beautiful and complete, and I was in unconditional love with her. I could not let anyone hurt her, not then, not ever.

Chapter 31

FIT OF RAGE

"Open the door, Prachurjya. I need to talk," I said, pounding on the door for the third time.

"We can talk tomorrow," he called back from the other side.

"I am sleepy."

"I am not!" I yelled, my frustration building.

It was hard to believe this was the same person I had once spent all my time with at the hostel. The room that used to feel like my second home, where we would hang out for hours, ignoring assignments and deadlines, was now closed off to me. The friendship we once shared felt out of reach, and the absence of that bond weighed heavily on my heart.

I kept knocking, harder and harder, almost on the verge of breaking the door down, when finally, Biswajyoti opened it. He stepped aside without a word, his face tense.

Prachurjya was on his bed, scrolling through his phone, not even bothering to look up.

"What do you want from me?" he muttered, his voice flat and distant.

I swallowed my frustration and stepped into the room, trying to keep calm.

"I don't want anything. I just… we can't keep going like this. We've been friends for too long to end up like this."

He cut me off, his tone cold.

"What do you want?"

I clenched my fists but forced myself to stay composed.

"Look, Prachurjya," I exhaled. "Let's forget what happened. Let's leave it in the past and start fresh. You have always been like a brother to me."

He scoffed, his indifference evident, and it took everything in me not to lose my temper and storm out of the room.

"I know you don't want to hear this," I sighed. "But we can still set things right, Prachurjya."

For a moment, he said nothing. Then, with a dismissive tone, he muttered, "Alright. What do you want me to do?"

He paused before adding, almost reluctantly, "I am sorry."

I felt a flicker of hope, surprised and amused at the same time.

"You don't have to apologise to me," I said softly.

"I am sorry too, for everything."

He nodded, then smiled gently and patted my shoulder.

"I missed you," I added.

"It's fine now," he said, his tone lighter.

"Chill."

"Glad," I replied, a smile creeping onto my face.

"Hey… if you could also talk to Kuhi. She is really upset. You don't even need to apologise, just… talk to her. Let her know that we are fine."

"Tell her it wasn't her fault."

He gave me a blank look but went on to pick up his phone. I felt a wave of relief.

"Do you want me to call her?" he said.

"No, wait," I blurted out.

"Let me do it… You only need to talk to her, that's all."

"Cool!" he said flatly.

I immediately pulled out my phone and dialled Kuhi. She picked up almost instantly.

"Hey," I said, my heart racing. "Prachurjya wants to say something to you."

I handed him the phone, my chest tightening. For a moment, I thought this could be the moment we all moved forward.

"Kuhi, hey," he began, his voice eerily calm. "I just realised you haven't been doing well, and maybe I am partly to blame for that."

Something felt off, but I held back, thinking it was just nerves.

"I am sorry," he continued, pausing for a beat before adding, "But you know what? You deserved it."

The words hit me like a punch to the gut, knocking the air out of me. My mind raced, trying to process what he had just said.

"You deserve all of it," he went on, his voice now dripping with malice.

"Sticking your nose where it doesn't belong. Who the hell do you think you are, Kuhi?"

The room seemed to go still, his words slicing through the air. I stood frozen, unable to believe what I was hearing.

Biswajyoti's jaw dropped open too.

"Let me tell you who you are," he sneered.

"A sympathy-craving, attention-seeking hypocrite. You thrive on messing up other people's lives, don't you?"

I felt the blood drain from my face. My heart pounded in my ears as I struggled to contain my anger.

"First, you try to mess up my life by setting me up with some random person just to boost your own self-esteem. And now you have the audacity to send your boyfriend over at midnight to feed your ego? Is that it?"

"Well, I am sorry, Kuhi Sharma. Happy now?"

My fists clenched and unclenched, a battle raging inside me, but the moment his words echoed in my head, I lost control.

"Enough!" I screamed, my voice shaking the room.

Before I knew it, I had slammed Prachurjya against the door. The rage inside me boiled over, and my fist connected with his face, landing a punch just below his eye. He dropped the phone and let out a cry of pain.

I didn't stop. I couldn't. I dragged him by the collar and shoved him out the door, rage blinding me. He hit the floor hard, his face already bruising.

Biswajyoti tried to intervene, but I pushed him aside, my focus entirely on Prachurjya. Blow after blow, I unleashed everything I had. Each punch was fuelled by all the betrayal, all the frustration, and all the pain that had been building up.

"How... could... you..." I screamed with each hit.

"How dare you speak to her like that?"

"Do you know what she has been through?"

Prachurjya's face was bloodied, his hands weakly trying to shield himself, but I didn't care. I wanted him to feel every bit of the hurt he had caused.

Suddenly, I felt hands pulling me back. As I looked around, I saw a crowd had gathered—my hostel mates, the warden, and even the Dean of Students' Welfare.

They dragged me away, and Prachurjya was quickly helped to his feet by some of the others. He was bleeding heavily, barely able to stand, as they rushed him off to the health clinic.

I stood there, panting, my knuckles aching, my mind racing. I knew there would be consequences. I knew my actions had gone too far, but in that moment, none of it mattered.

Then the Dean looked at me coldly.

"You are done for, you are expelled."

Those words hit harder than any punch I had thrown. The reality of it sank in slowly—in one night, I had destroyed everything.

In one night, I had lost my hostel, my semester, and possibly my entire future.

Chapter 32

BREAKING POINT

For some reason, everything felt surreal. It was like a terrible nightmare that I could not wake up from, but reality was beginning to set in. This wasn't a dream. In a few hours, daylight would come, and with it, perhaps the suspension letter that would mark the end of it all. My mind spiralled with a sea of thoughts. Missed calls from Kuhi, Ritika, and at least ten other numbers lit up my phone screen, but I wasn't ready to answer. Not because I was afraid, but because I had no answers—none that made sense to me.

Maybe I could have been calmer. Maybe I should have kept my composure. I acted without thinking. In that moment, it felt like the only way to defend her, even though I soon realised how reckless it was.

I cared for Kuhi in ways I didn't fully understand myself. Yes, I loved her—more than I have ever loved anyone. Loving someone that deeply can make you vulnerable, and sometimes it clouds your judgement. But when it's the right person, it feels worth the risk. And Kuhi was the right person—or at least, I thought she was.

At ten o' clock in the morning the next day after that horrific brawl, I was summoned to the Dean's office. As I walked in, I saw the Dean, my Head of Department, and the Assistant Dean seated across the room. They gestured for me to sit, and I took a seat, my heart heavy with anticipation.

"You two were always like a cup and plate, you were always together, everywhere you went," the Assistant Dean remarked.

The Dean scoffed at his comment.

"Explain why you did what you did last night," my Head of Department said calmly.

I remained silent. I had nothing to say—nothing that would justify my actions. Maybe I didn't even want to explain it.

"Alright," said the bespectacled Dean, dressed in his usual black coat, his thinning hair slicked back. He scribbled something on a sheet of paper, his expression cold. He glanced at me, his sharp eyes cutting through the silence.

"Destruction of hostel property… Assault on a fellow student… Creating a nuisance at midnight," he said, his voice stern.

"Not a very smart thing to do, was it, Mr. Madhav?"

I looked at him, then dropped my gaze again, unable to respond.

"If you don't speak in your defence, this will go severely against you," my Head of Department cut in. "You and Prachurjya have always been good friends. What could have led you to this? I don't understand…"

Still, I said nothing.

"Fine then," the Dean sighed, placing the pen down. "You may leave."

I stood up and walked out as quickly as possible, their words echoing in my mind: *"Destruction of hostel property… Assault on a student… Creating a nuisance at midnight."*

As I approached the hostel, I saw Kuhi standing outside, waiting for me. Her eyes were red, swollen from crying. It looked as if she hadn't slept at all. She looked at me, her expression a mixture of hurt and confusion.

"Why?" she asked softly.

"I don't know," I muttered.

"I asked you to mend things," she said, placing a hand on my shoulder.

"I don't want to talk about it," I replied, shrugging her hand away.

"Madhav," she whispered, her voice laced with concern.

"You didn't have to do that," she added.

"He is your friend, after all."

I couldn't take it anymore. I needed space.

"Not now, Kuhi, please," I said, my frustration boiling over.

"Madhav," she spoke again, her voice softer this time.

"I just want to understand, Madhav. Let me help you," she said, her tone filled with sincerity.

"Not now... Please go," I yelled. "I have had enough. He disrespected you, and I thought standing up for you was the right thing to do. If you see it differently, I don't know what else to say."

I stormed past her and into the hostel, leaving her standing there, helpless and bewildered. My phone buzzed again—it was Kuhi calling, but I ignored it. She wouldn't stop, though, and I eventually picked up.

"Kuhi, please," I said, my voice strained. "Give me some time. I'll call you back."

"Madhav," she said softly. "It's okay. Please talk to me."

"Kuhi," I growled, my patience thinning. "Just leave me alone."

But she wouldn't. She thought it was her fault, but I knew it wasn't. Still, her persistence was getting under my skin.

"I am waiting outside," she said. "I am here for you."

"Stop it!" I howled, my anger spilling over. "For God's sake, leave me alone, Kuhi! You've already done enough."

"I only went there because you had asked me to."

"I knew it was a bad idea, yet I went, and now that it has actually gone pretty bad, please just let me be."

"I do not want to talk about it. Let me be, I beg you. Just go away."

She paused, and for a moment, the line went silent.

"Alright," she whispered before disconnecting the call.

In a fit of frustration, I threw my phone across the room. My life felt like it was unravelling, and I wanted nothing more than to escape it all. I thought things couldn't possibly get worse, but deep down, I knew this was just the beginning—the beginning of the end.

I collapsed onto the bed, trying to escape reality. Soon, my mind slipped into a dream, taking me to a place far removed from the chaos of my life.

With one ball remaining and four runs needed, India finds itself in a dire situation. The final man, standing firm for three hours, must now face the ultimate test of skill and courage.

Madhav, ladies and gentlemen, is exhausted but determined. Can he pull off a miracle for his team, for his country?

Madhav is on 97. A boundary here will not only secure his century but the championship for his country as well. He has shown tremendous resolve today, but it all comes down to this one ball.

The bowler steams in, and Madhav locks eyes with him like a hawk zeroing in on its prey. He knows the stakes.

The ball is short, and Madhav goes for the pull—but it misses the bat and strikes him hard just below the neck. Jersey number 42 crumbles to the ground, and with him, so do India's hopes.

My heart raced as I shot upright, the dream's sting still fresh in my chest. Reality was even worse.

It took me a moment to realise it had all been a dream—a harsh reminder of how far I had fallen. I checked my phone after having picked it up from the floor. There was an unread email.

The end was finally there, just as I had feared.

Chapter 33

SHATTERED TRUST

Dear Student,

With deepest regret, we must inform you that you have been debarred from participating in the current and upcoming semester at the university. This decision has been made unanimously and in accordance with the violation of the University's Code of Conduct. You are also hereby ordered to vacate your seat in the hostel for a year, and you will no longer be able to participate in any university activities.

Please be aware that any further violations will lead to more serious consequences, including the possibility of expulsion.

Regards,

Nabin Pathak

Dean

Tezpur University

As I read through the lines, my heart sank. I knew this was inevitable after what I had done, but I clung to a faint hope for escape. No miracle arrived. I placed my phone aside and closed my eyes, trying to process it all.

Prachurjya was one of my few friends, and I had become his worst enemy. I had almost maimed him, and the realisation began to sink in. Tears rolled down my face. I thought I didn't care, but I did. Maybe he deserved it—maybe he didn't—but he was like a brother to me. Now, he lay in the hospital because of me.

I wanted to apologise. I wanted to undo everything. But this wasn't a movie, and sometimes, life doesn't go well. Mine was falling apart.

As I lay there, my phone buzzed again. I didn't want to answer any more calls, but when I saw Ritika's name, I paused. For some reason, I felt she might understand what I was going through. She had witnessed everything—our friendship, our mistakes.

"We need to talk," she said, her voice shaky.

"I guess," I replied.

"I should have listened to you," she said, breaking down.

"Ritika, are you crying?" I asked, alarmed. I had never seen her shed a tear before except for the time when I was at the hospital.

"Hey, what happened?" I said.

"I need to meet you," she said, her voice pleading.

"Now?" I asked.

"Yes," she said. "Please."

She hung up, and I stared at my phone, trying to comprehend what was happening. Ritika never showed her emotions like this.

I hurriedly put on some clothes and headed downstairs when my phone beeped again.

"Meet me at The Three Chefs. Please don't tell Kuhi."

It was an odd request, but I didn't question it.

I called Kuhi.

"Hi," she answered softly.

"Hey… I am sorry for how I behaved," I said.

"No problem," she replied gently.

"Can we meet now?"

"Give me some time," I said. "I need to visit the Dean," I said. "I'll call you once I am back, okay?"

"Okay," she sighed. "I love you."

"I love you too, and I am sorry," I said, though my heart was heavy.

I could have told her I was going to meet Ritika, but I wasn't sure why I lied. Maybe I didn't think it through; it was instinctive. I decided to tell her once I returned. The truth could wait for a moment.

I knew I had let Kuhi down too. She had stood by me through everything, and when she needed me most, I wasn't there for her, once again caught up in my own problems. I silently vowed to make things right with her, to bring back the smile I loved so much.

With that promise in mind, I made my way to 'The Three Chefs'. This was the place where everything had started to go wrong.

As I walked in, I saw Ritika sitting alone, her face covered with a scarf. My heart skipped a beat. This wasn't like her.

"What's wrong?" I asked as I approached.

She didn't respond. Instead, she broke down, sobbing uncontrollably. As she wiped her tears with her scarf, something caught my eye that left me stunned. Bruises—cuts, injuries, like she had been in a fight. My heart raced as I gently pulled her scarf away, dread curling in my stomach.

"What happened?" I whispered.

She buried her face in her palms, and I knelt beside her, gently rubbing her back.

"Ritika, please, tell me."

After what felt like an eternity, she finally spoke.

"You were right," she said, her voice cracking. "It's Rohan."

"What?" I said, stunned.

"Last night... we were at his flat, and he... he snapped." Her voice trembled. "He grabbed me, Madhav. He accused me of being involved with you."

I clenched my fists but stayed quiet, letting her continue.

"He wouldn't listen. He kept saying he knew something was going on between us. Then he... he hit me."

"He said he loved me all this while and he hurt me, Madhav. He hurt me…"

"He hit me, Madhav. He pushed me to the ground... I couldn't stop him, he overpowered me."

Saying this, she started sobbing and hugged me. She was inconsolable. People began to look at us, wondering what had gone wrong, but she kept crying.

A cold rage swept through me, my fists curling tightly. How could anyone do this to her?

"He will have to pay for this," I growled.

"No, please," she pleaded.

"You are already neck-deep in trouble. Don't do anything that makes things worse for you," she said, grabbing my hand.

I agreed reluctantly. Even though I wanted Rohan to suffer, the time wasn't right.

"We have to report this then," I said, my voice shaking with anger.

"No," she said quickly. "I don't want to involve anyone. My parents... they are extremely conservative. They would kill me if they found out I was at his flat."

I took a deep breath, trying to calm down.

"But we can't just let him get away with this," I said. "He has to be taught a lesson."

"Madhav, maybe he was the lesson," she said quietly. "I made a mistake, and now I am paying for it."

I didn't know what to say. I couldn't stand the thought of her suffering in silence.

"Okay, text him," I said. "Tell him you never want to see him again and that if he comes near you, there will be consequences. If I see him around you ever again, he will regret it."

She nodded; her eyes filled with tears.

"Madhav, please, don't tell Kuhi about this," she said, her voice barely above a whisper.

I hesitated but eventually agreed. "Alright. If that is what you want."

She smiled faintly, wiping her tears.

"Let go now," I said. "You've hugged me for an eternity, I need to breathe."

She playfully punched me on the ribs.

"So... suspended for how many years?" she asked softly.

"Just one," I laughed, trying to lighten the mood.

She wiped her tears again, this time with a faint smile breaking through the pain. There was a heaviness in the air between us, but the tension seemed to ease, if only for a moment.

"Idiot," she said softly, her voice regaining a touch of its usual strength as she lightly tapped my wrist. The gesture was small but familiar, a fleeting return to the friendship we used to share.

Chapter 34

THE FINAL NAIL

For hours, I had been trying to call Kuhi, but for some inexplicable reason, the calls wouldn't connect. At first, I thought it was a network issue, but as time dragged on, my concern deepened. She wasn't online, and my anxiety grew. With my impending hostel expulsion the next day, I knew I had to tell my mother. The thought of breaking the news to her was unbearable, but it was inevitable. She would eventually find out about my year-long suspension.

"Maa," I said when she finally answered the phone. It took immense courage to make the call; I knew I would need even more to deliver the full truth.

"Rubu," she replied. Her voice always had a way of making even the gravest problems seem manageable.

"Maa, there is something I need to tell you," I began, bracing myself.

"About the suspension?" she said calmly.

I was stunned. "How did you know?"

"Your Dean called me," she said. "It was hard to believe at first, but then Ritika reached out and filled me in on everything."

"Ritika?" I said, sounding surprised.

"I have never questioned your decisions or actions, and I never will," my mother continued. "That's how much faith I have in you, son. But this shouldn't have happened.

Come back tomorrow, but before you do, take the time to clear up the mess so that when you return, you have friends to support you.

Our actions have consequences, Rubu. In the end, it's our choices that shape our lives, so be sure to make the right ones."

"Take care, son," she said before hanging up.

"Wow… that wasn't bad at all," I murmured.

Just as I was about to try calling Kuhi again, Prachurjya's roommate, Biswajyoti, walked in.

"Hey," I greeted him.

"How are you?" he asked.

"Better, I guess," I replied.

He nodded.

"Look, Biswa, I am sorry for what happened last night. Prachurjya was my best friend—probably still is—and I shouldn't have done what I did."

"I understand," he said. "But he kind of had it coming, though not in that way."

I tried hard not to laugh.

He chuckled.

"By the way, where is Kuhi going? I saw her a few hours ago outside. She had a big bag with her and handed me a letter, requesting me to deliver it to you at exactly 11.11 p.m. Although I am afraid I am a minute or two early," he added with a smile. "It's not your birthday, is it?"

I didn't respond. My mind was racing, trying to piece together why Kuhi had left a letter with him. He handed me the envelope, and I took it with trembling hands, a pang of dread hitting me.

"Alright, I'll leave you to it," he said. "See you around."

I nodded absentmindedly and shut the door behind him. My hands shook as I unfolded the letter, feeling a surge of dread and anticipation.

Madhav,

By the time you read this, I will be gone. Don't try to call me; the number won't connect. I always wondered what being in love would feel like, and then I met you. I never imagined that you would become so important to me, to the point where your happiness meant everything to me and seeing you sad made me feel desolate. In such a short time, you became a significant part of my life. I know I was important to you too, but Madhav, remember what they say: "Try as much as you want to, if it's not meant to be, it never will be." You felt like home, and I was willing to stay in that home forever. Remember when you said you would swim oceans for me, that you would always be there? I believed that. You were my support system, and now that I feel that support dwindling, I feel I have no right to linger.

Remember the day at the movies when you told me you loved me? I wished time would freeze there. When I rested my head on your shoulder and you kissed my forehead, it felt like all my troubles had vanished. Now, all that's left are memories. Remember, it's not your fault. I chose to leave.

"I can't afford to lose you. Not again. If I do, I won't know what to do, I'll be gone... far away."

I am sure you remember these words. I think the time has come, Madhav. Just know that I will always be there for you. Don't try to contact me; this is a decision I made, and maybe I never deserved you. I love you. Somewhere, someday, maybe.

I hope you read this at 11.11. They say, "all good things start at 11.11." I hope this is the beginning of something wonderful for you too.

As I read, the tears began to blur the ink on the page. The reality that Kuhi was no longer in my life started to sink in. The reasons behind her departure were unclear, but the fact that she thought I no longer loved her was heartbreaking. I could accept the suspension and even expulsion but losing Kuhi felt like losing a part of my soul. I tried calling her once more, but the same automated message played: *"The number you are trying to reach is not available, please call again later."*

I was shattered, not just by the loss of my career and friend, but by the loss of the girl who meant everything to me. It felt like my entire world had crumbled. My *Girl in White* was gone, and it was the final nail in the coffin of everything I wanted, all the dreams I once had.

Chapter 35

THE LAST LEAF

You know what happened yesterday? We had a get-together—all of us, after so long, together in the same place, walking down memory lane. I wasn't planning to go. I knew you wouldn't be there, and honestly, I didn't want to see anyone. But my wife... she was excited, so I had to.

I paused, staring at the half-empty cup of coffee in front of me.

Divya was there too. You remember her, don't you? We talked about everything—about you, about us—about how things were back then, fourteen years ago. Can you believe it? Fourteen years since you left, and not a day goes by without me wishing I could see you one more time.

I let out a deep breath, feeling the familiar weight of those years.

You never explained why you left. You said I lost interest... or at least that's what I assumed. But even after all these years, I don't really know. Had you known I would be sitting here, writing this fourteen years later, would you still have gone?

I picked up my pen again, memories flooding back.

For years, I have resisted tracing your path. I have tried to move on, but every night, I stare at the same photo before I sleep, the one I captured on your instant camera on the day of your birthday. I know I have lost you, Kuhi, but how do you forget the person who taught you the meaning of love?

Sure, we aren't together anymore. But you weren't someone I could replace. I have tried and failed. I still love you. I wish I could tell you that someday. Last night, I reread our old texts—the ones before the big Inter Hostel final when we first met. I miss you. I wish I could time travel, go back to the day you left, and persuade you to stay.

You know, I am still angry. You left, but you gave me no reason. How could you do that to me? You thought it only hurt you, but it hurt me too, and it still does—every single day, it has kept hurting every single day for fourteen years.

You said, 'If something isn't meant to be, it never will be, no matter what.' I held onto hope, thinking you would come back. But that day hasn't come in fourteen years. I don't even know what I would do if I saw you again. Apologise? For what? For something I wasn't guilty of. Would you apologise for abandoning me like that?

I thought fourteen years was enough time to forget and forgive. But it's not. I have tried and failed every single time. Even now, when I hear your name somewhere, my heart skips a beat, hoping it is you. I don't know why I still love you, but the truth is—I always have.

Maybe you were selfish, thinking it only hurt you. But God, it hurt me too. So badly. You would never know.

I still remember the first time I saw you—walking into class in that white sweater, with those wired earphones. I didn't know it then, but at that moment, you became my Girl in White. And even thirty years from now, when we are both in our mid-sixties, you will still be my Girl in White.

I stopped writing. My hand hovered over the yellowed pages of the diary, trembling slightly. The words I had never said out loud still felt raw, even after all these years. Kuhi had vanished from my life, but the wound never healed. How could it, when she gave me no explanation?

Fourteen years. Fourteen years of wondering every night, why she had gone away.

I closed the diary and placed it gently on the table beside me, leaning back in my chair. The room around me was silent, except for the distant hum of life carrying on, as it had all these years.

"Madhav, can you help me fix this regulator?" Ritika's voice came from the other room, breaking my thoughts.

"Yeah, I am coming," I called out, forcing myself to focus on the present. I stood up, stretching my stiff muscles, and walked to the window. Outside, life seemed so normal. But inside, I was still a prisoner of the past.

I had been married to Ritika for six years. Through everything—every high and low—she remained by my side, patient and understanding. She knows about Kuhi. She knows I've never fully let go. But Ritika never complains. She's my anchor, the one who stayed. And now, we have Aaradhya, our two-year-old daughter, the light of our lives.

As I was about to leave the room, my phone buzzed. I glanced down at the screen.

"Hi, Madhav."

I stared at the unknown number, confused. Could it be a wrong number? But something made me reply,

"Hey, who is this?"

"Madhav, are you coming?" Ritika called again.

Another text came in.

"You don't know me. But I know you. Meet me at Café Bistro at 5 p.m. today. It's about Kuhi."

My heart stopped for a moment. I reread the message, feeling the air leave my lungs.

Kuhi? After all these years?

"Who are you?" I typed, my hands trembling.

No response.

"Madhav?" Ritika's voice was closer now. I hadn't even noticed her walk in. I quickly locked the phone and slipped it into my pocket.

"Yeah, I am coming," I muttered.

"What's wrong?" she asked, her eyes searching mine.

"Nothing, just work stuff," I lied.

My heart raced. Who could this person be? What do they know about Kuhi? Why now, after fourteen years?

I finished helping Ritika with the regulator, but my mind was somewhere else. What if this was a prank? Or worse, what if it wasn't? What if, after all these years, I was finally going to get the answers I had been waiting for?

I had always wanted those answers, but I never anticipated how I would feel when the day finally arrived.

By the time I arrived at *Café Bistro*, it was fifteen minutes to five. I parked across the street and sat there for a moment, staring at the entrance.

Fourteen years of silence; fourteen years of pain.

I stepped out of the car, my hands shaking.

As I approached the entrance, I took a deep breath.

"Fourteen years," I whispered to myself, pausing before walking inside.

I had no idea what I was about to walk into, but I knew one thing for sure: my life was going to turn upside down just like the time she walked through the door for the first time, except that this time I was the one walking through a door.

Chapter 36

THE GIRL IN WHITE

I had been sitting there for thirty minutes, drinking coffee after coffee, growing increasingly impatient. The longer I waited, the more I wondered if this was some kind of prank. Frustrated, I dialled the number again, but, as before, it didn't connect. The situation mirrored that fateful day fourteen years ago when I had dialled a number time after time, but it wouldn't connect. I was on the verge of leaving when a familiar face walked through the door. I struggled to remember where I had seen him before.

He approached, his stubble and unkempt hair reminiscent of someone from my past. "Can I sit?" he asked.

"Well… yeah," I said, still struggling to remember who he was.

"Not able to recognise me, are you?" He smiled.

"I am the one who texted you."

For a moment, my heart sank. I had hoped—perhaps unrealistically—that Kuhi would walk in and smile at me. Instead, this man had arrived.

"I am Rohan," he said. "Rohan, the so-called ex-boyfriend of your wife, Ritika."

My shock was palpable. This was the same Rohan who had assaulted Ritika. And now, years later, he was sitting across from me in a café, as if nothing had happened. Ritika wouldn't have been pleased.

"Is this some kind of joke?" I demanded.

"Oh no," he said quickly. "This is not a joke."

"What do you want?" I asked, trying to control my anger.

"I'll explain everything," he said.

I nodded; my breath uneven. I was struggling to grasp the situation.

"It was Ritika," he began.

"What do you mean?" I asked, confused.

"She was always in love with you," he said. "Why do you think Kuhi left? She left the university, gave up her career, and walked away from you... Doesn't that seem strange?"

My heart raced. "I don't understand."

"Ritika and I were never really in a relationship," he continued. "I was in love with her, but she used that to manipulate you."

"I don't believe you!" I said. "Ritika said she was happy with you. You assaulted her! If I had the chance, I would have reported you."

"How dare you hurt her?" I added.

"Then why didn't you complain?" he asked, a smirk on his face.

I hesitated. "Because her parents wouldn't…"

"Ritika had no parents," he interrupted. "She was raised by her uncle and aunt."

I was stunned.

"They passed away when she was in the sixth standard," he said. "How could you not know?"

I faltered. "They passed away a year after she graduated."

"No," Rohan said. "That is not true. She has been alone for much longer."

I felt numb. Ritika had never spoken much about her parents. It had never crossed my mind that she had lost her parents at such a young age.

"So, what does this have to do with Kuhi?" I asked, desperate for answers.

"Everything," Rohan replied. "We never had a real relationship. Ritika asked me to pretend we were together to make you jealous. When that didn't work, she staged the assault herself. That was her masterstroke."

I could hardly believe it.

"She convinced you that I was the one who hit her," Rohan said.

"And let me show you something."

He pulled out his phone and played a video. It was of me and Ritika hugging on the day I was suspended.

"But she was crying. I was just consoling her," I said, shocked.

"Did Kuhi know that?" Rohan asked. "For all she saw, you were hugging Ritika. I am sure you didn't tell her about meeting Ritika that day."

I felt my world crumbling.

"And remember that text you told Ritika to send me?" Rohan continued.

"What text?" I asked.

"That text where she was supposed to tell me to stay away from her," Rohan replied.

"Yes," I said.

"She didn't send it to me. She sent it to Kuhi instead, but with a twist. After watching the video and receiving the text, Kuhi was devastated."

"She texted Kuhi, claiming you both liked each other, and asked her to stay away from you. She told Kuhi that you got hit on the head during practice because you were texting her, and that your expulsion was due to Kuhi's interference. She even made Kuhi believe it was her fault that you assaulted Prachurjya. It was all her doing."

"She meticulously planted seeds of doubt in Kuhi's mind, one by one."

"In fact, Ritika was also the one who told Kuhi not to say anything about her father's death, worried it might make you lose focus on the tournament. That innocent girl didn't hesitate for a moment before shouldering all her pain alone."

"And remember how, while you two were at *Niribili* during her internship, you suspected someone was hiding behind the bushes? I was there, taking pictures."

"Ritika used all of that to break Kuhi, making her feel like she was the problem and that she didn't belong here."

"That poor girl was already shattered after losing her father, and what Ritika did, triggered the kill switch. She left as if she had never existed in any of our lives."

Tears streamed down my face. Kuhi must have been heartbroken beyond words.

That is what Kuhi meant when she wrote, "*I hope this is the beginning of something wonderful for you too*" in that letter fourteen years ago. It all started to make sense. She believed I was in a much better place with Ritika, and that must have shattered her.

"Prachurjya was also fooled, believing Ritika's story," Rohan continued.

"She convinced him that you belonged to Ritika, not Kuhi. And that idiot believed her. Of course, he would think that way; you and Ritika were the only friends he had."

"Turns out that brawl… it was partly because of Ritika too," Rohan said.

"If it hadn't happened, things might have turned out differently."

I was overwhelmed.

"I… I can't believe this," I said.

"You know," Rohan began, "I'm sorry. I've lived with this guilt for fourteen years. When Divya told me that she still saw love in your eyes for Kuhi at the get-together, I just couldn't carry it anymore. I knew I had to tell you the truth. Even if it changes nothing, maybe it will ease your pain, knowing what really happened."

I was devastated. I couldn't believe what I was hearing. Could Ritika—my wife, my best friend—really have done this? She had always been by my side, always there for me. She wouldn't hurt me. Or would she?

"But if you loved Ritika, why did you get involved in this?" I stammered, my voice barely a whisper.

"That's the whole point," Rohan said, his tone heavy with regret. "I was in love with her—madly in love—and I thought that if I helped her, maybe she would fall for me too. I was wrong. I was a fool."

His words struck me like a thunderclap. Kuhi didn't deserve any of this. She only deserved love.

"I think I should go," he said, not even looking back to say goodbye.

As the door clicked shut behind him, a profound silence enveloped the room. I felt the weight of his confession settling heavily on my chest, like a stone sinking into deep water. My mind raced with the implications of his words, a whirlwind of emotions leaving me breathless.

With each passing moment, the gravity of the situation settled in, and I felt an ache where hope had once lived.

As I drove home that evening, I wiped away the tears. After fourteen long years, the truth had finally surfaced. But was it the truth I had been hoping for? Probably not.

I had the answers I had desperately wanted every single day of my life. I thought knowing them would bring me peace, but the truth was cruel.

I was better off not knowing any of it.

Just then, my phone rang—it was Ritika.

I stared at the screen as her photo popped up.

"Hey," I answered.

"Hi!" she said sweetly. "Can you pick up some baby food on your way home? We are out, and Aaradhya might wake up soon."

Aaradhya—our two-year-old daughter.

"I will," I said.

"Thanks. Love you!" she said.

"I love you too," I said, though my mind was a whirlwind of thoughts overwhelming me.

I looked at the photo of Aaradhya on my lock screen and whispered, "My little angel."

I typed a message to Rohan: *"Let's pretend this conversation never happened."*

I drove to the nearest store to pick up what Ritika had asked me to. What Ritika did was wrong, on many levels, but maybe she did it out of a misguided sense of love. I had a family, and that was what mattered most. As for Kuhi, her words echoed in my mind: *"If it's not meant to be, it never will be."*

And maybe she was right. Maybe this was how the story had to end.

The Girl in White walked out of my life just as she had entered it—nonchalant and spectacular—turning my world upside down both times.

EPILOGUE

Aaradhya turns four today; can you believe how swiftly time flies? It feels like just yesterday I was holding her in my arms in the maternity ward. She was a blessing then, and she always will be. In just a few days, she will be starting school. She has your nose—did I ever mention that? I can already imagine the day when you meet her and say, "Hey, did your dad give you my nose?"

She is so much like you. She has a passion for books and insists that I wash my hands before touching her textbooks. She can be a bit bossy, though, just like her mother. The other day, she asked me about this diary. I told her it was about The Girl in White. She thought it was a television show. In a few years, she will grow up, and she will turn out to be just like you—spending time at the library, surrounded by more books than people.

There will come a time when this diary will be set aside, for she does not need to read what is written inside. She is my daughter, and I love her so deeply—probably more than I ever thought was possible.

This is the final chapter, and with it, a goodbye from me. Aaradhya has a fondness for white too; sometimes I wonder if she is a part of you. Goodbye, Kuhi. You will always be my Girl in White.